NEXT IN THE SERIES, COMING SOON:

Bad Boys in Boston
It's just business, never personal.

Crash Landing
Public pressure, private pain.

Del Chatterson is also **Your Uncle Ralph,** writing for entrepreneurs:

The Complete Do-It-Yourself Guide to Business Plans
"It's about the process, not the product."

Don't Do It the Hard Way
*"A wise man learns from the mistakes of others,
only a fool insists on making his own."*

THE DALE HUNTER SERIES:

No Easy Money

You never win playing by the rules...

First in the series of Dale Hunter crime novels, No Easy Money is an explosive mix of crime, cash and computers in the 1980s. Dale Hunter is a young entrepreneur in the computer business under threats of violence from the Montreal Mafia. He wants to survive and not play by gangster rules, but it will require courage and creativity and the support of some new friends. Somebody is going to get killed.

Simply the Best

It may be simple, it's never easy

Dale Hunter is back in business, but so is Gino Boncanno. Hunter has already had to save himself from a murder attempt by the gangster, Boncanno. Now his new partner in Taiwan introduces him to the Triads and their smuggling scheme into the U.S. The danger escalates and Hunter still has to save his family from the murderous plans of Boncanno. It may be simple, but it's never easy.

Merger Maniac

Some offers have to be refused

Third in the series of Dale Hunter crime novels, Merger Maniac is the story of how Dale Hunter tries to make his business bigger to survive against competitive threats in the rapidly evolving computer business of the 1980s. He's looking for new partners, but has to escape the aggressive and violent Montreal Mafia, who are seeking a new partner in their money laundering schemes and making very persuasive offers.

READER REVIEWS OF
NO EASY MONEY

"I liked it a lot! And I was there, in the computer business of the 1980s. I loved the interaction with organised crime in Montreal and the protection racket. I'm telling all my friends and I bought two more copies for my sons for Christmas. Bravo Del, very impressive!"
Gilles Gaudet (Montreal, Canada)

"Very enjoyable read. I enjoyed the book and all the characters around a business enterprise, a real business challenge that leads an Entrepreneur down a road he shouldn't go, but does! Waiting not so patiently for the next one."
Chris Murray – Amazon.ca Review – 5 Stars –

"Welcome to the '80s Business World. I love how the story flowed and how the intensity continued to increase, keeping you reading through to the very end. This story takes you back into the thick of the 1980s business world and all of the difficulties that came with it. Dale is a smart and talented businessman with a company growing almost faster than he can handle. However, this growth and success

draw him deeper and deeper into a nightmare, from being forced to buy protection to working with a loan shark. There's extortion, coercion, and backroom deals that made this story exciting. Mobsters, dirty cops, and even dirtier businessmen keep you on the edge of your seat until the very end, making for an intense and exciting read. Enjoy the ride! It's a fast one!"
Amanda Leeber (USA) – Amazon.com Review – 4 Stars

It may be simple,
it's never easy

SIMPLY THE BEST

BY DELVIN R. CHATTERSON

SIMPLY THE BEST
It may be simple, it's never easy.

By Delvin R. Chatterson

ISBN-978-0-2288-1390-3 HC
ISBN-978-0-2288-1389-7 SC
ISBN-978-0-2288-1391-0 EB

Edited by Allister Thompson, Ontario, Canada.
Cover design by Caroline Teagle, NYC, USA.
Author photo by Mario Carangi, Montreal, Canada.

Published by:
Uncle Ralph's Publishing Empire
(Division of 146152 Canada Inc.)
&
Tellwell Publishers Inc.

Dedicated to enlightened entrepreneurs everywhere,

trying to do better for themselves and their families, their employees,

customers and suppliers, their communities and the planet.

Also dedicated to the families,

friends and lovers of entrepreneurs.

SIMPLY THE BEST

Who's who

Dale Hunter– Currently retired, 1980s entrepreneur and Owner of 3D Computer Products.
Susan Bowness – Dale Hunter's wife
Sean & Keira – Dale Hunter's son & daughter
Frank "The Fixer" – Former Somalian refugee, now working both sides of the law in Montreal
Detective Hélène Bourassa – Montreal cop & Frank's girlfriend

Sammy Wong – Owner of Chung-Wai, a manufacturer in Taiwan
See Yeung – Triad leader in Taipei, Taiwan
Kim Phat & Sung Phat – Triad leaders from California

Gino Boncanno – Montreal gangster
Pietro Lombardi – Primary enforcer for Gino Boncanno
Tony 'Stack' Di Staccato – New York Mafia boss
Pat Cametti – Mafia boss of Stack Distribution
Dino Mancini – Casino Owner in Las Vegas
Paulo Renaldi – Mafia boss of Ottimo Financial Services

Marie de Carlo – Receptionist at 3D Computers
Guy Tremblay – Technical Manager
Patrick Jensen – Sales Manager
Rick Petrie – Bank Manager
Mack Stevenson – Sales Rep for STB, a manufacturer in Texas
Jim Annapoulis – President & Owner of ABJ Data Products
Bobbie Brydon – Owner of BIG Distribution in Montreal

MEMORIES IN A HAT

"Jeez Dad, that hat must be thirty years old."

Dale Hunter's son, Sean, was looking at a faded orange baseball cap hanging on a hook at the back of the front hall closet in Dale's condo.

Sean had just arrived and he was reaching into the closet to hang up his jacket when he saw the hat. It was a remarkably neat, well-organized closet. Heavy winter coats were hanging in a back section with light summer jackets in front. Boots and shoes were arranged below. A golf bag and two pairs of golf shoes were tucked in a corner.

The hat had once been a bright orange, but was now only a faded reminder of its original neon brilliance. Stitched in black above the peak of the cap was the logo, STB, with the slogan, *Simply the Best*, written beneath it.

"Yeah, it does go back thirty years or more," said Dale. "STB was one of our video card suppliers at 3D Computers."

Dale lived alone in a high-rose condo in the downtown Montreal residential neighbourhood of Nun's Island. He had retired from his business and moved into the city from the suburbs a decade earlier. His son, Sean, also lived in a condo downtown, about fifteen minutes away. This evening, they were on their way out for dinner together at a favourite restaurant, *Le Baton Rouge*.

Dale remembered the company, STB, from Texas and their sales rep, Mack Stevenson, a big gregarious Texan. Like other suppliers visiting Montreal, he was always more interested in visits to the strip clubs than the business meetings. Montreal had a Sin City reputation from the 1950s that was still an attraction for some visitors. Dale kept the *STB* hat among other souvenirs of the "good old days" in the computer business of the 1980s. He called back to Sean down the hallway. "That's the hat I wore for my marathons, remember? The fluorescent orange made it easy to find me in the crowd."

"Oh, yeah. We knew we were never gonna find you at the front of the pack."

"Hey, a little respect for the old man, please. At least I was never last. Hell, in New York there were nine thousand runners finished behind me."

"Yeah, and twenty-five thousand ahead of you."

"OK smart-ass, you force me to remind you that you were never that fast either, even as a teenager. Dead last in a 10-kilometre race one spring, I remember."

"Yup, that's me, built for power, not for speed."

Sean was a solid, strongly built thirty-eight year-old. He had played on the offensive line for the Concordia Stingers football team at university and he had loved to run into his opponents and hit them hard. Otherwise, he was still the same studious, gentle personality that he had been as a boy.

"Good slogan, *Simply the Best*," Sean remarked.

"Yeah, I like it too," said Dale. "Keep it simple, be the best. They didn't really live up to their slogan, but we had no real problems with STB. The horror stories all came from other people."

"Horror stories? I don't remember any horror stories," said Sean. "I thought it was all good times in your business, back then. Good times for the whole family, as I remember."

Yeah, well you didn't hear all the stories. We never told you or your sister about the gangsters coming after us with murder on their mind.

Out loud, Dale said, "Maybe someday I'll tell you all the stories. Meanwhile, enjoy your cushy job and big bucks in the corporate world. All you need to worry about there is navigating through the corporate politics. That's the part I hated most about working in a big company."

Sean replied, "Yeah, it's no fun putting up with all that crap. I'd like to just do the work, have some fun and get paid a shit-load of money for doing it, of course."

"Now there's a career plan," said Dale.

"I'm not ready yet to take off on my own and become an evil, rich entrepreneur, like you," said Sean, smirking. "Maybe with a little more experience, someday soon, I'll take a look at starting my own business."

"Then you'll find out for sure," said Dale, "whether or not you have to be evil to get rich. You'll discover you have to make some tough choices and it's hard to be the last of the good boy scouts."

"Sounds like you're trying to explain some bad shit you got into that you haven't told me about, Dad."

"Nope, not me. I managed to stay honest and keep it legal," said Dale with a flick of his eyebrows. "Most of the time."

His mind flashed back over memories of the gangsters interfering with his business and dragging him offside a few times. "Whatever you do in business," he said, "be careful choosing your partners, as well as your suppliers and customers. They can all lead you into places you shouldn't go."

"You trying to talk me out of going into business for myself?"

"Not at all. It's very appealing in many ways. I'm just saying make good choices and try to control your own destiny. Avoid being dependent on anybody else. Try to succeed like my old friend, K.Y. Ho, at ATI Technologies. He started his company from zero at about the same time as me, but he went on to build it into a world leader with his own high-tech products, designed, built and marketed himself. Very impressive story. He eventually sold his company for about five billion dollars and was able to retire at fifty-five."

"Jeez. And all you've got to show for your years of hard work is an old hat from STB?"

"Sorry about that. Not so good for your inheritance, I know. But I already told you and your sister not to count on it. You're right, though, it'd be nice to retire with that kind of cash in the bank." Dale's mind wandered back to the obstacles that had knocked him off track. "More stories you'll hear, someday," he said.

There were some good years, but there were other times we just worried about staying alive. A brief shudder shook his shoulders as Dale remembered the phone call that had shaken him up so badly that afternoon, thirty years ago.

He was in his office at 3D Computer Products and the call had been from his wife, Susan, at home.

He picked it up and suddenly he heard a man's rough voice on the line. "Listen to your wife, Hunter. Do as you're told and nobody gets hurt."

It hadn't been that simple.

=======

Part 1:

Partners Helping Partners

1.

It started with another phone call to Dale. This time he was at home and the call was from his business partner, Sammy Wong, in Taiwan.

It was after dinner and Dale was in the family room watching the evening news on TV with his wife, Susan. The kids were upstairs in bed. Their daughter, Keira, was already asleep, but her older brother, Sean, said he had some reading to do before turning his light out.

Susan had taken the phone call and called back to Dale from the kitchen. "It's Sammy," she said, holding the phone out from the wall and covering the mouth-piece with her hand.

Sammy Wong was the owner of Chung-Wai, the primary manufacturer and supplier of computer monitors for Dale's distribution business in Montreal.

Dale and Sammy were also joint owners in a computer products distribution business in New England. They regularly phoned each other and tried to make their calls during business hours at both ends, but it was not always possible with the thirteen hour time difference between Montreal and Taipei.

"OK, I'll take it upstairs," said Dale. "Sorry, but he's already at the office. it's tomorrow morning in Taiwan. Must be something important."

Susie nodded. She had had her evenings interrupted before by Dale's work and it wasn't just Sammy from Taiwan. She had learned that owning your own business meant always being available to business partners, or customers and suppliers and employees. They all had Dale's phone number at home.

"Call me anytime," he told them. And they did. *He thinks easy access to the owner is good for the business,* thought Susan. *He needs to be reminded sometimes, that easy access to the husband and the father is also good for the family.*

She knew that Dale couldn't control all the interruptions and sharing an active family life with their kids, Sean, aged eight and Keira at six, was important to him too.

Dale took the phone in his upstairs office and waited to hear the click, as Susan hung up in the kitchen. The background hum of the long distance call echoed off Sammy's voice on the line.

"Sorry to bother you at home, Dale, but we're already hard at work here at Chung-Wai. The next shipment for Boston is nearly ready for you, but I have a special request on this one."

"OK," said Dale, "is there a problem?"

"No problem," said Sammy, "just a special request. It's the usual 40-foot container full of 14-inch colour monitors, but for this shipment, I'm including six boxes that are not for you. They're a special delivery for, uh, another custtomer, in New York."

"OK. So you're short-shipping me by six units?"

"Not exactly. The invoicing and all the customs paperwork will still show 448 units of CHW-1428 computer monitors at the current price. The six boxes will look the same as all the rest, but you need to separate them from the monitor shipment. We'll make sure you can find those six boxes when you unload the container in Boston. They'll be in the second to last row at the back of the container. We'll identify each of the boxes with extra QA stickers. You know, the square yellow labels from Chung-Wai Quality Assurance that show the model and serial number. The stickers will be marked as inspected, marked OK and signed off. I'll sign these stickers myself, so you'll know they're the right ones."

Dale was starting to feel more uncomfortable by the minute, as Sammy Wong explained what was required of him in Boston.

"Jesus Sammy, what the hell are you smuggling in this shipment? I don't want any part of it. They take smuggling very seriously in the U.S. We're risking getting the business shut down and getting me thrown in jail with this plan."

"Dale, I need you to do this for me or some really bad things will happen here. You'll suffer the consequences, too."

"What are you talking about, Sammy? Are you threatening me now?"

"No, of course not. We're business partners and friends, Dale. I just don't have any way out of this, without asking for your help. Please don't ask too many questions. I'm under serious threat from the Triads here and you really don't want to know any more about it. I just need you to do this for me, please. I wouldn't ask if I had any choice."

Dale said nothing as Sammy continued.

"Just do as I ask without any questions. You don't need to get involved."

"But you're asking me to get involved, Sammy. I'll have to sign off on falsified paperwork, unload the dirty goods and then hand them to your friends in New York. That's what you're asking me to do, right?"

"Yes. It's not complicated. Just follow my instructions when you receive the container. Call the people in New York and they'll come to pick up their shipment. Hand over the six boxes and you're done. Then you can wash your hands of it and walk away."

"Do you even know what's in the boxes?"

"Yes, we repacked the stuff into Chung-Wai monitor boxes here last night."

"Sammy, we're trying to build a good, legitimate business together in Boston and this is a big step in the wrong direction."

"I took the first steps a long time ago, Dale."

Sammy sounded tired of the whole fiasco and reluctant to cooperate with the Triads, too. "I'm trying to keep you and others out of harm's way," he said. "But the Triad boss here has his hooks into me pretty deep. I have to play along. It's best if you don't know too much and just do as I ask. We're partners helping each other out, right? I got you out of a jam with the crooks in Montreal, now I need you to keep me out of trouble with these guys. If we do it right, nobody gets hurt. We just have to play along, until they let us off the hook somehow, later." His voice faded into silence.

"I don't like it Sammy, but it sounds like I can't refuse."

"Like I said, we have no choice."

Dale continued to object and reminded Sammy of the risks to them both, but he finally agreed to accept the mystery boxes in his shipment before hanging up the phone.

I'm not convinced we couldn't make better choices, but Sammy's committed to this plan, it seems. The problem is these guys in Taiwan and New York aren't likely to let him stop after one shipment. Especially if we deliver what they want.

Maybe I should just screw it up so badly, they'll never ask us to do it again. But I don't want to make matters worse for Sammy. The Triads have a reputation for being pretty ruthless about getting what they want.

And Sammy's right. He did get me out of a jam that could have been a disaster when the Mafia was squeezing me for more than I could handle. He was a friend when I needed one, so now I have to return the favour.

Dale remembered the threats of violence from Montreal gangsters and the Mafia back then.

But Sammy wasn't the only friend to help me out of that mess. Maybe it's time to call on Frank again, Frank the Fixer.

Dale came back to the family room and dropped back into his La-Z-Boy lounge chair facing the TV. Susan looked at him for a moment, then reached for the remote control and turned it off. Dale continued staring at the blank screen.

"Dale!" Susan said sharply.

He jerked his head up, blinked and frowned at the blank TV. He turned and looked at her.

"What?" he said.

"Never mind what," she said, "I've lost you to Sammy, it seems. What's he got you worrying about this time?"

"He's just being Sammy, getting too creative in Boston again."

"Creative is OK, when you do it, Dale, but Sammy worries me."

"Well, sometimes we get dragged into trouble, no matter how hard we try to avoid it."

"So what's he up to this time?"

"Nothing to worry about, Susan. Just a little extra shipment into Boston he wants me to look after."

"Jesus, Dale. You don't want to get caught doing anything illegal in the States. They'll put you away and we'll never see you again."

"No, no. Really. I'll keep away from anything illegal myself, as much as I can. I don't want any more trouble either, but I owe Sammy. He did step up with enough cash to get us away from the Mafia loan sharks, not long ago, you remember. Now he's got his own sharks to deal with in Taiwan and he needs my help. We're in business together in Boston and he's supporting it without hesitation, so I have to step up this time. I'll try to end it as quick as I can."

"Please, Dale, we don't need to get into any more trouble with criminals. Last time, it almost got you killed and they got too close to all of us. We don't want more of that nightmare."

"Don't worry, this will stay in Boston and I'll get out of it as quick as I can."

He reached for the TV remote. "Let's get back to what's going on in the rest of the world." The TV lit up and he turned away from Susan.

"Don't tell me not to worry," said Susan. "I need to know you won't bring it home this time."

She scowled at Dale, who was no longer looking at her. He nodded silently, but kept his thoughts to himself, as the TV news intervened again.

Believe me, I'll keep this as far from the family as possible. We've all had enough encounters with the gangsters in Montreal and I'm not looking for more trouble from them now in Taiwan or the U.S.

2.

Dale Hunter was riding the wave of personal computer products that washed over North America in the 1980s and he was enjoying the success of his rapidly growing business.

It's been a wild ride, he thought. *And I'm still managing to stay on top of the wave. Not bad for a small town kid from the Rockies with no surfing experience.*

Dale's company, called 3D Computer Products, specialized in computer display products and sold to personal computer retailers, clone builders, systems assemblers and network installers from his distribution centre in Montreal.

Dale had started the business in 1984. He pushed hard and took more business risks than his original partners from Toronto could tolerate, so Dale bought them out to continue his rapid growth independently. The partners, Don Leeman and Doug Maxwell, were competent and ambitious businessmen, but Dale thought they were too cautious and holding him back. They all respected each other and accepted their differences. They still retained a close business relationship and they continued to share suppliers and sales territories across Canada.

A key factor contributing to Dale's early success was his proprietary EXL brand of computer monitors. The monitors were sourced from low-cost manufacturers in the Far East; Chung-Wai in Taiwan and Korea Computer Systems in Korea. The EXL branding allowed Dale to distinguish his product line from other computer display products flooding the market. All the smaller Canadian distributors were trying to sell their products against the strong competition of the better known multinational brand names like HP, Toshiba, Hitachi, NEC and Sony.

Dale had started his business after losing his executive position at AES Data, a failing computer manufacturer in Montreal. AES was unable to transition into the personal computer market and would fade into oblivion by the end of the decade. Their specialized word-processing equipment was more expensive and less versatile than the desktop personal computers from Apple and IBM, as well as all the low-cost personal computer clones. Talented technicians and entrepreneurs were successfully building and selling computer products from their garages and basements all over North America.

Dale had the satisfaction of being among those small independent entrepreneurs who were winning business from the big corporations that had used and abused them all, in the past. He had been attracted to the challenge of running his own business, ever since leaving his original profession of engineering and earning his Master's in Business Administration, an MBA, at McGill. His subsequent forced departure from AES Data, and the substantial severance package he negotiated, provided the opportunity and the funds to pursue his entrepreneurial ambitions.

He was amazed and delighted by his rapid success in business and he was confident in the affirmation of his talents as an entrepreneur. He was also pleased to see Susan relieved of her concerns for the family's financial security after the unexpected loss of his job at AES Data.

Dale pushed himself and his staff to exceed even his high expectations and he was willing to take the necessary financial risks to pursue his objectives with creativity, but he was stubbornly determined to play by the rules. That meant accepting his obligations and honouring his commitments without any excuses, though he knew his competitors and other striving entrepreneurs felt less constrained. They found it easy to accept the risk of getting caught offside and rationalized that "Everyone's doing it" and "You'll never win playing by the rules."

Dale refused to accept that logic. He declined to take cash under the table or to cheat on his taxes. He was deliberate in meeting the sometimes onerous regulatory requirements put on his business and perversely, he found it even more satisfying to win at the viciously competitive game of business without breaking the rules.

Sometimes I have to bend the rules and play in the grey area. But I do it my way, dammit.

Dale was doing over ten million a year in sales in 1988. He was enjoying all the perks that came with his financial success. He had never experienced it before. He did not have a wealthy family history and came from a solid middle-class background. His father had been a tradesman and his mother a school teacher.

The first challenges to Dale's business from the criminal world came about two years earlier. Thieves broke into 3D Computer's warehouse in the night and stole almost $200,000 worth of computer products. Nothing had ever been recovered and the crooks had never been caught.

During the investigation, Dale met a Montreal Urban Community Police Detective named Pierre Forsey who seemed capable and effective, but still failed to solve the crime. Later, when the gangsters came back demanding protection money and threatening violence against Dale and his family, he had called on Detective Forsey again.

Unfortunately for Dale, it turned out that Forsey was dirty and on the payroll of Gino Boncanno, the ruthless gangster who was behind both the robbery and the protection racket. Detective Forsey failed to do anything useful, so Dale decided to take matters into his own hands.

Forsey had tried to stall by introducing Dale to someone called Frank, Frank the Fixer. The introduction was intended as a diversion to keep Dale from discovering Forsey's connection to Gino Boncanno, who wanted to demand increasing amounts of protection money from Dale. Forsey was benefitting from his share of the action.

As Dale began to suspect that Forsey was looking after his own interests more than Dale's, he arranged to meet the mysterious Frank the Fixer. He discovered that Frank was an imposingly large young man and a former Somalian refugee only eight years in Canada, who had learned to survive in the tough underworld of Montreal.

It had taken time for Dale and Frank to get to know and respect each other, but they had become friends and worked together to extricate Dale from the threats and intrusions of Boncanno. Frank, the street-wise Montrealer, was more capable of dealing with Montreal gangsters than Dale, a small-town kid from the Canadian Rockies.

With Frank's help, Dale had managed to fend off Boncanno and his gang of thugs by seeking the protection of another Mafia family. Eventually, he had survived the attacks on his business and his family.

It was the worst year of my life and I never want to go back into that world again. What the hell is Sammy getting me into now? His half-million was good to get me out of the clutches of the Mafia loan sharks, but it was never meant to be a ticket back into business with more criminals from Taiwan.

I know it's hard to avoid the crooks. And there are a lot of greedy and unscrupulous people trying to get rich in the computer business. But Sammy's call for help with smuggling into the U.S. goes too far. I'll have to end this as soon as I can.

I hope Frank has some ideas.

3.

Dale's introduction to smuggling of stolen computer products started with the phone call from Sammy Wong to his home in Montreal.

Two weeks earlier, Sammy had been in his office at the Chung-Wai factory, a few miles outside of Taipei. It was at the end of a typically hot, humid day in Taiwan. The large second-floor windows were closed to keep the heat and the polluted air outside. The spacious corner office looked out over an irregular array of low flat-roofed buildings in the industrial park. The pale light of dusk produced no highlights in the monochromatic scene. Only a few illuminated signs and exterior lights on the buildings added some colour and contrast to the shadows.

Sammy Wong was a small, middle-aged man with jet-black hair and bright eyes constantly scanning his surroundings through steel-rimmed glasses. He radiated energy and confidence and had a reputation for being eminently personable and charming in a social setting, but sly and calculating in business.

He sat high in the large swivel chair at his desk, smartly-dressed in a white shirt with a red tie pulled tightly at his throat, in spite of the uncomfortable heat. Sammy was not looking out the windows.

He was looking intently at the bulky figure overflowing the armchair in front of his desk, See Yeung, well known as the local boss for the Triads. The Triads of Taiwan were a major link in the international Chinese crime syndicate that was most prevalent in Hong Kong, but well-established in major centres around the world.

See Yeung's presence dominated the room. His fleshy arms rested on the sides of the sofa-sized chair and his huge belly dropped between his splayed knees. He wore a multi-colour floral-patterned silk shirt that would have been a billowing tent on a normally large man, but was tautly stretched over the truck-tire sized rolls of fat around his waist. His loose fitting, pale beige linen pants were pulled up under his shirt and the wide pant legs hung above his bare feet bulging out of leather sandals the size of frying pans, pressed to the floor.

See Yeung's shaved head glistened with sweat. The ceiling fan above him in the centre of the room spun silently without any effect, except the occasional flutter of papers on Sammy's desk.

Sammy was perched like a miniature Chinese doll on a pedestal and See Yeung was slumped into place like a giant toad from another planet, about to flick out his tongue to grab Sammy like an insect and swallow him in one gulp.

They were speaking Mandarin. See Yeung patted his head with a folded white handkerchief and spoke in a soft voice that seemed incongruous to his girth and the aggressive scowl on his face.

"We have been very reasonable, Mr. Wong, not asking for more money to keep your business safe," he said politely. "Now we need your cooperation to assist us with a shipment to the United States. You have one or two containers a month going to your business in Boston, is that correct?"

"It's not exactly my business," said Sammy, "I have a partner there, who's from Montreal. He only visits Boston about once a month and I was there only one time, over a year ago."

"Well then, you will have to get your partner to cooperate, too. It is not a very complicated request."

Sammy frowned, knowing that Dale Hunter would not be very cooperative, once he knew who was behind this "not very complicated request".

Sammy had been forced to include the Triads in his business soon after he expanded production into the new larger factory for Chung-Wai and started making regular shipments to America. It was hard to hide his prosperity and it attracted criminal predators demanding cash for protection to avoid their threats of violent disruption to his business. He chose to meet their expensive demands in order to avoid any trouble. There was no way for Sammy to fight back.

Now, See Yeung and the Triads were dragging him further into their criminal activities and he didn't see a way out of that either.

"What is it that you need?" Sammy asked. "Can we at least make it appear like a normal business transaction?"

"You can handle it any way you like," said See Yeung. He started to heft himself out of the armchair. "I'll let you know when we have the goods ready for shipment."

Sammy heard from them with a phone call about five days later. He was told to expect a delivery at the factory that evening. He asked one trusted employee to remain with him to receive it.

Three men arrived after dark in a small van and delivered several large unmarked cardboard cartons. They insisted that Sammy take a close look at the contents and count the boxes inside.

"Make sure they all get delivered," said the leader of the three. "See Yeung does not like surprises. When will they arrive in Boston?"

Sammy confirmed the container would arrive in about three weeks.

"OK," the man said, "Have them call this number in the States when it's ready for pick-up."

He passed a note to Sammy, then left the two of them to repack the product into computer monitor boxes and prepare the shipment for Boston.

4.

During their previous encounters, Dale got to know more about Frank the Fixer. He learned that his real name was Faysal Mohammed Abou and he had come to Montreal as a seventeen year-old Somalian refugee.

Faysal, now called Frank by everyone in Montreal except other Muslims and his sister, had survived the vicious civil war and tribal violence in Somalia and escaped to Canada where his survival skills also helped him avoid being recruited into the street gangs of Montreal. He was now enjoying the good life of a young, single man with money in the big city.

Frank was recognized as the Fixer by people on both sides of the law. He was very skilled at playing the crooks and cops against each other without getting caught in the crossfire.

Dale had not been in touch with Frank for about six months. Frank guarded his privacy, but he and Dale met occasionally. They liked and respected each other and learned new perspectives through the windows of their very different worlds.

I'd rather not call on him again, thought Dale. *But he is definitely better than me at beating back the criminals. Maybe he has friends in*

Boston who can deal with this smuggling business. I need to extricate myself from these Taiwanese gangsters somehow.

Dale had called Frank and they agreed to meet at one of their preferred spots downtown, Ben's Delicatessen on the corner of De Maisonneuve and Metcalfe. The restaurant was famous for its smoked meat and the hustler atmosphere that made it the go-to diner for decades. The walls were covered with signed celebrity photos from the visiting stars of hockey, stage and screen, including Rocket Richard and Jean Beliveau, Frank Sinatra and Fats Domino, John Wayne and Marilyn Monroe. The muted green and beige décor with the melamine and chrome tables and countertops never changed and neither did the menu.

Dale and Frank were seated at a small table by the windows facing De Maisonneuve Boulevard. They settled over the large plates of thinly sliced smoked meat with a token covering of rye bread beside a small paper cup filled with coleslaw. French fries and two large dill pickles, cut lengthwise in quarters, were on separate side plates.

"We should meet for a round of golf, instead of all this heavy food we're indulging in again, Frank," said Dale. "There's a nice little nine-hole course in Dorval, near the airport not far from my office. Might be a good way to spend a couple of hours in the sunshine and still talk business."

"No, thanks," said Frank. "I don't play golf. I think it's boring and a waste of time, trying to hit a little white ball down the fairway and into a tiny hole four hundred yards away."

"C'mon Frank, it's a great game! You learn to manage strategy and execution, have a plan and make it happen. It's simple, just hit it long and straight and then gently roll a curling putt into the hole. Power and finesse, just like business, you have to master both. And golf develops character and mental toughness. It also reveals character. You'll learn who cheats or can't control their temper. Might be good for you, Frank, to play a little golf."

"Nope, it's not for me. I prefer sports with more body contact. That helps to reveal character, too."

"But that's another good thing about golf, you don't have to watch out for anybody whacking you over the head or body-checking you from behind. So you're saying you'd rather join me on the ice for some hockey, then?" That was Dale's other favourite sport and he had played at a high level through university.

Frank looked amused. "Are you kidding me? I'm from Africa, man, no ice there and I never learned to skate. Football is my game. Soccer, as you call it."

"Oh yeah? Are you any good at that? My son, Sean, could use a little coaching."

"Of course, I'm good at it. You learn fast, playing against other tough, angry Somalian kids on a dirt road with a half-inflated ball. You have to get good at it or find another game to play. But I'm not much of a coach. No patience, especially with these soft, privileged Canadian kids. I'd be too hard on them. Even your son, Sean."

"Maybe that's what he needs," said Dale. "Anyway, no golf, I guess."

He fiddled with the remnants on his plate, then pushed it aside. He reached forward to re-arrange the salt and pepper shakers and the yellow plastic condiments basket filled with packets of ketchup, mustard and relish.

Frank watched and waited for Dale to return to the conversation. He had seen Dale's obsessive neatness before and learned to watch patiently bemused, but without comment. The first time he had noticed it was at Bennie's Restaurant, another favourite spot for their meetings. Dale had been continuously rearranging the condiments tray, the salt and pepper shakers and the utensils on the tabletop between them, until Frank had finally questioned him. "What's with all the fidgeting, Dale?"

"It's not fidgeting," Dale snapped. "I just like to bring a little more order into this messy world we live in." He didn't like to be reminded of his compulsive habits. It was just his way of removing himself for a moment to let his mind meander before coming back to the conversation.

"So," Dale said, "Let's get back to our favourite pastime, sorting out the criminals in my life."

Frank nodded and smiled. "Now, that's what I'm really good at."

"OK, let me tell you what I'm up against with the latest complications from my partner in Taiwan."

Dale explained what he had heard from Sammy Wong about the special shipment that was now on its way, arriving soon at the warehouse in Boston. "I'd like you to be there with me when it arrives, so we can make arrangements to deal with it. You're better at this stuff than I am, Frank."

"OK, but why me? Why not just call the cops and have them waiting for the New York guys, when they show up."

"You know we can't do that. We're already involved in the dirty work ourselves. Both Sammy and I are in deep shit, if the cops get involved. You're my guy, Frank, when we get into this kind of trouble. I've learned to trust you more than the cops, who haven't always been very helpful. I don't even want to meet them in Boston or New York. I may be getting better at working in the grey areas, but I'm counting on you to help me out here."

Frank shrugged and smiled, accepting his role as the occasional Fixer for both gangsters and good guys. He was confident. *I'm sure I'll find a way to look after this*, he thought. *Maybe have some fun and make a little money on the side.*

Dale was reflecting on their different backgrounds and how they ended up fighting crime together in Montreal.

"Remember, I'm just a small-town kid from the Rockies and we never had any big-time criminals there. Even in Vancouver, where I was at university, there were just a few pot heads getting into minor mischief. Of course, I just kept my head down avoiding the distractions. No time to get into any trouble."

"Ah, you were such a good boy, Dale. Now, remind me again, why did you come to the sinful, dangerous city of Montreal? You sure you didn't come here just for the cute French-Canadian girls, like me?"

"I already had a cute wife and kids on the way. You're the one with the cute French-Canadian girlfriend, not me."

"She's got more Irish-Mohawk than French-Canadian in her, if you really want to know," said Frank. "Hélène's got all the bases covered and she's perfectly bilingual. She should be in politics."

"Well, you're a lucky guy. Take good care of her and it might even last for you." Dale paused to remind himself of his good fortune to have found his future wife and partner for life, Susan, at university.

"To answer your question," Dale said, "I came here first and foremost to get my MBA at McGill. As an Anglo from Western Canada, I was fascinated by the mix of French and English. Even if they sometimes clash, it makes Montreal an interesting and exciting place to live. Sometimes, it gets out of hand. I arrived right after the infamous FLQ crisis of October 1970, when the separatists went from blowing up Canada Post mailboxes to kidnapping a British diplomat and murdering a Quebec Cabinet Minister. That took a while to recover from, but now we all get along pretty peacefully and just yell at each other in the newspapers or in Parliament."

Frank nodded, acknowledging his own introduction to Canada.

"The only violence in Montreal, when I got here in '79, was at the Forum hockey rink. Especially when the Canadiens played the Boston Bruins or the Philadelphia Flyers. Man, that was something to see. Sticks and gloves flying, blood everywhere. And it's just a game!"

"Yeah, the FLQ terrorists had settled down by then and were locked up or exiled to Cuba. Hockey violence is still in the game, though it isn't really necessary. It's just to entertain the fans, especially those new fans in the U.S. who have no experience with hockey. The goons don't add much to the game, but they seem to be part of the attraction for some people."

Frank returned to Montreal's political history. "I heard about your FLQ terrorists and the crisis in 1970," he said. "But the FLQ was pretty tame compared to the terrorists and gangs in Somalia. Violence there was a lot worse than bombs and kidnapping and murder. It was brutal tribal warfare, anything and everything to terrorize and eliminate the enemy. Nowadays, they call it ethnic cleansing or genocide, but those are just big words for the brutal facts of life back home and it hasn't changed much since I left."

"Sounds like Hell on earth," said Dale. "It must have been hard to lose your parents in the conflict. How's your sister doing, since you got her out and settled here in Montreal?"

"She's still wasting her time, enjoying the good life, instead of studying hard to get a better life At least she's safe. It's good to have her close by, even if she wishes her big brother didn't check on her quite so much."

Frank smiled at the thought of his sister complaining about his attentiveness, when they both knew she loved him for it.

"I'm sure she'll be fine, Frank. Especially with you keeping an eye on her."

Dale drummed his fingers on the table. "Now, let's get back to my little problem. I need your help with this shipment coming to Boston."

After explaining what Dale knew about the smuggled goods in the shipment from Sammy Wong, Frank agreed to come down to

Boston as soon as Dale could confirm when the container would arrive at the warehouse there.

Frank added that he had connections in Boston and New York who might be able to help Dale out of this jam. "I'll make some calls and find out who'd like to jump into a good fight with the Triads."

Dale started to relax and see some hope of passing this smuggling business off to somebody else.

"Thanks, Frank, sorry to have to ask for your help again, but the criminals keep showing up. I hope it's the last time. Then we can just enjoy lunch and a beer and be done with them."

What Dale didn't know was that he had another problem with the criminals.

Gino Boncanno still wanted to kill him.

5.

Gino Boncanno still had revenge for Dale Hunter on his mind and he was not going to forget it. Hunter had made him look like an incompetent fool and caused the Renaldi Mafia family to wipe out his business and send him into hiding.

Boncanno had originally been introduced to Hunter by one of his henchmen, Jacques Talbot. Talbot had threatened Dale and demanded protection money, but he was working on his own account, which got him into a lot of trouble with Boncanno. After that was straightened out, Gino cranked up the cash demands and the threats against Hunter and his family. The mounting pressures were more than Dale could handle and pushed him into a deal with the Renaldis for protection from Boncanno and for financing to save his business.

Boncanno was enraged by getting bumped out of the picture and had tried to have Hunter killed by Talbot. Frank had intervened and Talbot had bungled the attempt on Dale's life. To end any further threats from Boncanno, Frank had the Renaldis destroy Boncanno's Luna Rossa Restaurant and his headquarters at the adjacent Club Calabrese. In the nighttime attack they had shot up the place and killed one of Boncanno's bodyguards. Gino, however, had managed to escape the firestorm alive and disappear into seclusion.

He was never going to forget that Hunter had caused him all these troubles. He couldn't let it go. He was not going to fight the Renaldis. They had too much power and would be willing to finish the job on him, if he ever got in their way again.

Gino obsessed over Hunter as the target for his revenge. It had been almost two years since the settling of accounts with the Renaldis. Gino was now back in business on the familiar fringes of organised crime. He had quietly reorganized his gang of thugs and was again using them in his protection racket, robberies and break-ins. The Renaldis seemed to be ignoring him, so he had decided it was time to take another shot at Hunter.

He would normally have used his old enforcer, Jacques Talbot, but Talbot had screwed up on the first attempt and was currently sitting in a jail cell after being convicted for manslaughter in another killing. In that case, a sleazy computer dealer named André Lebeau, who was buying stolen computer products from Boncanno, had been killed in his apartment. Talbot was sentenced to seven years for second-degree manslaughter and was in the Saint Vincent-de-Paul Federal Penitentiary outside Montreal.

After the attack on his organisation, Gino Boncanno had moved in with his brother in Saint Léonard, an Italian neighbourhood in the north-east suburbs of Montreal. Gino was there with his wife, Maria, and their young son, Antonio. When the conflict had settled down, Gino sold his Luna Rossa Restaurant and the Club Calabrese property that was attached to it. Both buildings had been severely damaged in the shoot-out and subsequent fire and the new owners had contractors working on reconstruction.

Gino did not want to be seen anywhere near those premises. He had set up his new headquarters in a back-room of the Restaurant Vida da Vinci on Saint Laurent Boulevard in the Little Italy neighbourhood not far from his brother's home. He and a few of his associates were now doing business together and generating lots of cash to indulge in their preferred vices again.

Gino Boncanno was quite conservative in his choice of indulgences. His preference was simply a good red wine and a large plate of pasta, sufficient to maintain his rotund figure and satisfy his vigorous appetite. Gino was short, dark-skinned and well-rounded from his large bald head with the trimmed fringe of white hair to his fat belly tightly wrapped in the vest and jacket of a wool three-piece suit.

Boncanno was a nasty, vindictive man, who thought of himself as a gentleman Mafia ringleader, not the small-time, two-bit hood that the Montreal Mafia families thought he was.

Gino was sitting at the desk in his office at the Vida da Vinci Restaurant. In front of him was Pietro Lombardi, a tall skinny man with long, lank brown hair and dark-rimmed eyes.

Lombardi did not have the stereotypical muscular build of the bodyguards Gino usually had around him, but he had a languid fluidity and blank emotionless face that made him even more menacing and hinted at the ruthlessness he would be quick to demonstrate, if the victim needed convincing. He was Gino's most effective enforcer and Gino was explaining his plan for revenge to Lombardi.

"I think the best way to get to Hunter is through his family," he said. "Hurting them will hurt Hunter more than anything else. In the process I want him to know that I am settling all the old scores. And he finally loses."

"What about the Renaldis coming after you again," said Lombardi, stretching out, crossing his long legs in front of him and folding his arms across his chest. He didn't look bulkier, just more relaxed, waiting for Gino to explain what was required.

"The Renaldis have forgot about Hunter by now and I'm not bothering them at all." Gino leaned back into his chair and pressed his fingertips together in front of his vest. "Hunter is all alone for us to take care of. I think maybe kidnapping his wife or one of his kids would bring him to us carrying a big bag of cash and exposing himself. Then we can finish him off. That would be a good ending, if you ask me."

"I dunno, Gino, kidnapping is already serious stuff. Now you're talking murder? The cops might not be so willing to stay out of your way, if murder's on your mind."

"Don't worry, I still have good connections with the cops. I'm sure they'll give me space to do this without any interference. If we do it right, they'll never even know what happened."

"I hope you're right." Lombardi sat up and leaned toward Gino. "So, what's the plan? Let's get on with it."

6.

Dale was having a good start to his day at home in the quiet suburbs of the West Island of Montreal. Susan and the kids were having breakfast on the fly, rushing back and forth to bedrooms and getting ready for school.

Both kids were in a private elementary school nearby and wore uniforms with grey slacks or skirt, white button-down shirts, black oxfords and a blue blazer with the red and green coat of arms of the Kirkland Academy on the breast pocket. There was no school bus service for them to take to the private school, so Susan shared car-pool duties with other Kirkland Academy parents. Today was her turn to drive.

Dale decided he had time for a run around the neighbourhood this morning, before going to work. He came downstairs wearing a T-shirt, with *Never give up* scrawled across the front, black polyester shorts and his favourite running shoes with a large green Nike swoosh on the grey webbed side of each foot.

He did a quick round of kisses and good-byes. "Have a good day at school, sweetie. Keep up the good work, Sean. I won't be home for dinner tonight, Sue, I've got a visitor from Texas and he'll want the usual tour of the clubs tonight, I'm sure."

"OK, just don't drink too much before driving home," said Susan, kissing him on the cheek and squeezing his arm.

Dale went out through the garage after filling his water bottle and tucking it into the pocket at the back of his jogging belt.

It was a short jog down the tree-lined street of two-storey houses built in the 1960s style of brick and fieldstone with aluminum siding and set back from the street behind neatly landscaped front yards. Dale left the neighbourhood and ran out to the sidewalk that led past the commuter rail station and under the tracks and Autoroute 20 to the south. On the other side, he jogged through a neighbourhood of larger homes by the shore of Lac St. Louis and continued west on the paved shoulder of Lakeshore Boulevard.

It was a relaxing run in the warm early-summer sun and he felt the tightness and stress leaving his body with each passing kilometre. He scanned the horizon across the lake through the bright green leaves to the blue sky beyond. He allowed his thoughts to roam from the business challenges of the day to their planned family activities and the current political issues and news headlines. The headline on the morning paper that he had picked it up from the front step and tossed in the front door, read "PM still fighting the Liberals on Free Trade and GST."

Dale thought they were both good initiatives by the Conservative Prime Minister, Brian Mulroney. Free trade with the U.S. would help the economies of both countries and make it easier to do business across the border, as well as reduce costs for consumers and give everyone access to more choices. *Hard to argue against that win-win for everybody. The Liberals fought hard against Free Trade in the campaign of '84, crying about loss of sovereignty to the powerful giant south of the border and they're still beating that drum. But Mulroney won the election and negotiated the deal with President Reagan, so now he wants it ratified. Seems reasonable to me.*

The concept of a Goods and Services Tax was even more complicated and controversial for Mulroney to sell to the Canadian electorate. The GST would be a value-added tax like they had in the U.K. and Europe and would replace the long-standing Federal Sales and Excise Tax. Mulroney argued that the GST would be simpler and more equitable as it would apply uniformly to all goods and services. It would also be more transparent, since it would be added to the invoice price before payment and not buried in the cost like the Federal Sales and Excise Tax. It would be clear to all Canadians exactly how much tax they were paying on every purchase. That turned out be the flaw in Mulroney's approach.

From the time the GST was finally implemented in 1989, Canadians were constantly reminded of the combined federal and provincial sales taxes on every invoice and sales slip that amounted to almost fifteen per cent in some provinces. It allowed the rationalization that it was finally too much and justified avoiding it, by any means possible. Usually, that meant doing deals for cash, no invoice and no tax collected or paid. It was illegal, but once again, "everybody does it."

Dale completed his running circuit and arrived home after about forty-five minutes. His T-shirt was now soaked with sweat as he stretched out and cooled down leaning over the picnic table on the back patio. After a brisk hot shower and a fast breakfast, Dale poured a large cup of coffee into his EXL travel mug for the drive to the office.

Before leaving, he ensured that everything was neat again in the kitchen. He arranged his dirty dishes and juice glass in the dishwasher, rinsed the coffee pot and filter into the sink, put them back in the coffee maker and squared up all the appliances on the counter top.

As he drove to the office about twenty minutes east on Autoroute 20, his mind returned to business and he ran through his agenda for the day. He knew the STB sales rep from Texas was bringing with him some complaints about 3D Computers not meeting their sales targets. Dale was going to have to respond strongly to protect his exclusive distribution contract.

The office and warehouse for 3D Computer Products was located in a modern industrial park near Dorval International Airport. The airport would be renamed twenty-five years later as Pierre Elliot Trudeau International, in keeping with the naming of Toronto's airport after Prime Minister Lester B. Pearson. Dale was at the office when his guest arrived by taxi from the airport.

Mack Stevenson, the sales rep for STB from San Antonio, Texas, was now seated opposite Dale at the small round conference table in his corner office. Mack fit the image of a big Texas cowboy, without the Stetson hat or cowboy boots, but with the blue jeans and the pearl buttons on his denim shirt. He was sprawled comfortably in the chair with his Western-style leather-trimmed sports jacket draped over the empty chair beside him.

"Your exclusive contract for Eastern Canada, Dale, has a sales quota of a hundred-and-fifty thousand dollars to be met within two years. You're a long way from that. Sales to date have been pretty weak, as you know."

"But Mack, as you know, STB is simply *not* the best. It may be a good basic video card that sells for only $99, but everybody prefers to pay more for the ATI-Graphics Plus at $129. The resellers make more and so do we, so there isn't much incentive for any of us to push STB."

"Yup, I know," said Mack, "you Canadians really love yer ATI, just because it's a Canadian company."

"Actually it's because they have really good product at a great price. We are proud they're Canadian, though, and winning big in the market. We're trying to do better for you too, Mack, just be patient a little more before you cut us off or introduce another distributor. We'll put some specials together with our EXL monitors and push hard through the fall. That should make a difference. The resellers will get busy again when everybody's back to school and back to work. It's always slow through the summer."

"Sounds like a plan," said Mack. "I know it ain't easy, Dale, and ATI is tough to beat. Just doin' my job bein' hard-ass and putting a little pressure on yuh."

Mack leaned over the table to speak more quietly. "Now let's get down to the best part of my visits to Montreal. Time for the strip clubs! Yer girls here are great."

Dale laughed. "OK, at least we can do that for you, Mack. But it's only four o'clock. Let's get you checked in at the hotel and go for an early dinner, before we meet up with your Montreal girlfriends."

"Great! You can't sell our product worth shit, Dale, but at least you take good care of me. I think you'll be good for another year."

"All right. Give us a chance and we'll show you we can sell even more of those crappy STB cards. Let's come up with a serious plan to do better, but it can wait 'til tomorrow."

They packed up and left the office. Mack was staying at the Airport Hilton, so Dale took him there to check-in and then they headed into the city. They went from the airport toward downtown on the Decarie Expressway and pulled into the Rib-'n-Reef for dinner. Over steaks and beer, they chatted about news in the computer industry and the sudden rise of Dell Computers in Austin, Texas.

"Hard to believe," said Dale, "Michael Dell started the company as a 19-year old student building computers in his dorm room at university. American entrepreneurs," he nodded approvingly, "Very impressive."

"Yup, he'll soon be another young multi-millionaire, like Steve Jobs at Apple Computer over in Silicon Valley. There's hundreds of 'em in Texas and California and New England, maybe Canada too, trying to get rich, but most won't last two years before they go belly up."

Michael Dell's success was based more on his innovative business model than on any innovative new computer product. Contrary to the standard approach of most manufacturers who sold to distributors who then sold to the computer retailers, Dell Computers sold directly to the end-user customers, both corporate accounts and individual consumers. They were taking direct orders from everybody on their toll-free 1-800 phone lines and delivering through UPS or the Postal Service.

"It's pretty radical," said Dale. "The computer resellers hate the concept because they're losing the customer and the profit margins."

"I know," said Mack, "But we don't hate 'em. They're not far from us in Austin, Texas, and they're currently our biggest customer. The retailers are definitely getting squeezed out, though, one way or another. Apple is talking about opening their own exclusive retail stores and bypassing the distribution channel, too. The big boys are gonna bump us all out of business one day soon. We better make hay while the sun shines, Dale. It ain't gonna last."

Dale nodded his agreement. *The big guys keep getting bigger and buying each other out to reduce costs and it only makes it harder to win against them. Their prices keep getting lower and they still spend a fortune on marketing to drive all the customers to their brand names. Mack is right, 'this ain't gonna last.' I've got to work fast to get my money out before the inevitable crash comes.*

"OK, Mack, too much doom and gloom. You're going to ruin the evening. Let's get out of here and check out the girls downtown."

"Helluva good idea," said Mack. "Let's go."

Dale signalled the waiter, "*L'addition, s'il vous plait,*" and paid the bill.

They continued down Decarie Expressway into the city centre, parked underground at Place Ville Marie and strolled along Saint

Catherine Street to the flashing neon sign announcing *Club Chez Paris* above a doorway outlined in incandescent bulbs. The large framed and illuminated posters on both sides of the door proclaimed "*Danseusses toutes nues*" with graphic photos of sexy naked dancers, making translation unnecessary.

One of the hefty, well-tailored bouncers at the door peeled off two Free Drink coupons. "Come on in, gentleman, the girls are beautiful and they're ready to rock 'n roll, just for you."

Dale led Mack in and up the stairs. It was still too early for the usual crowd, but Mack didn't notice. He was soon enthusiastically cheering on the flow of drinks and the parade of strippers on stage a few feet from their table.

It was not Dale's preferred locale for an entertaining evening. *I hope this helps our negotiations tomorrow morning and he's not too wiped out to be any good to me, after all this booze. He does get excited about these girls strutting their stuff. I find it depressing. I wonder if their fathers know what they do for a living.*

*****

Dale was back at the Airport Hilton at eight thirty the next morning. Mack was waiting outside the hotel lobby and told Dale he'd already had a good breakfast and enough coffee to wake him up. He was beaming with good humour and didn't appear at all hung-over.

"Let's get this wrapped up this morning before lunch," he said, "so I can make my flight to Toronto at two o'clock. There's a guy there making big promises to do great things for STB. Are you sure your partners in Toronto don't want our product before I sign him up?"

Dale watched him drop his small suitcase into the trunk and squeeze his long frame into the front seat of Dale's two-door BMW, then sit in beside him.

"Appreciate the offer Mack, but my partners in Toronto are very focused on monitors and don't want to get into the price wars and low margins we're up against on video cards. I work them into bundles and package deals for our resellers, so it's harder to compare on price and that seems to work. I'm happy for the incremental revenue, but we need your help to make it easier. Let's talk over another coffee at the office."

They spent the morning at the small round conference table in Dale's office and went through a pot of coffee. They shared ideas on marketing and the competitive positioning of STB relative to ATI and other popular video cards, especially the low-cost no-name cards imported from Taiwan and Hong Kong that were most often installed by the personal computer clone makers. Most of them were obsessed with chasing the lowest possible price on every component and were less concerned with performance or reliability. They were often techies and computer geeks, who just loved to play with the technology. They got into building computers and running a business only because it seemed easier, and was definitely more fun, than finding a job.

Since it was so easy to get into the computer business, there were too many competitors, especially at the retail level, all fighting for the same eager customers. The competition was ferocious, and for most resellers, their primary sales tactic was to continuously chase prices downhill and try to sell for less than anybody else. It drove them all to operate on very thin profit margins and many of these businesses did not last long.

Low-ball retailers were not Dale's preferred customers and he had to be cautious with them to avoid the risk of not getting paid. Disappointments and surprises were unavoidable and he had been burned by a few.

His preferred customers were those who were more competent businessmen, who understood the technology, as well as how to run a business. They were easier to persuade that other factors, like quality, reliability, customer service and technical support, were important to their business. These were the factors that helped Dale win their business, since he did not often have the lowest price.

Dale and Mack Stevenson finished their meeting and concluded the negotiation of STB issues in time for Dale to drive Mack back to the airport before twelve.

After he had returned to the office and tidied up his conference table, Dale went down the hall and tapped at the office door of his Sales Manager, Patrick Jensen.

"Hey, Patrick, I just made a new deal for us with STB and I'd like to meet with you and Guy to work on a sales plan. Are you free tomorrow afternoon?"

"Yeah, I can be free for a meeting then, but you know STB is hard to sell, Dale. I hope you didn't make any big promises."

"Not too big for you to handle, Patrick. I have confidence in you. I gave them an order for five hundred cards a month, starting this month and growing to fifteen hundred a month next year. Let's work on that plan tomorrow."

He turned away and went back to his office, smiling to himself as he noted the look of shock on Patrick's face. They had not sold more than two hundred cards since signing with STB in January.

As Sales Manager, Patrick Jensen was responsible for a team of four sales reps at 3D Computer Products. Guy Tremblay was the Technical Services Manager, responsible for product support and technical services, including training the sales team on new products. The two managers were both valued employees, but they did not always work well together. Their personalities and management styles didn't mesh at all.

Patrick was ambitious and protective of his turf, pushing the sales reps to meet sales objectives and follow his direction on sales tactics. Guy was a meticulous, methodical technician. He tended to look down on the sales staff, whom he thought were overpaid and under-educated in the technologies they were selling.

It made the working relationship a challenge for Dale to manage and he often had to stroke both their egos to facilitate their cooperation on joint projects.

When they met the next day, Dale set the agenda. "OK guys, we have a new sales objective with STB at five hundred units a month. Not that big a deal, but adding about fifty thousand a month in sales. My real objective is to get us up to fifteen hundred STB cards a month to make it worth our while, but let's prove ourselves at five hundred, then I'll go back to work on the pricing. Our prices and margins will be better immediately, because they've already reduced our cost."

"Those sales numbers are very ambitious, Dale," said Patrick. "STB is not that well-known. It can't compete with ATI on performance and it's over-priced against the cheap imports."

"I'm not hearing your usual energy and enthusiasm here, Patrick," said Dale. "We know all those objections. What we need is a good sales plan that targets the right customers and positions the product correctly. Let's start with the resellers who don't sell on price alone and don't rely on a recognized brand name to make the sale for them. Find resellers who know how to sell like we do. I know it's harder, but it leads to more loyal long-term customers. People appreciate our expertise, our reliable products and our strong customer service and support. That's what we do best and we need to work with customers who operate the same way. We're not talking about *Joe Sous-sol* working out of his basement who can't afford to pay for an office or *Johnny Slash-for-Cash*, the sleaziest retailer in the city pushing crap out the door in large quantities at low prices. Those are not our target customers, for STB or for anything else we sell, for that matter.

"So let's make a pitch to the customers that we already know, who are a better fit." Dale continued. "Let's go after the corporate network installers and high-end clone makers like Phoenix Systems and Canacomp, here in Montreal, or Civil Systems in Ottawa. I know we have customers like that elsewhere. Who else would be good prospects for STB, Patrick?"

Patrick was starting to buy into the plan and looked thoughtful.

"We have *Cyber-Systèmes Informatiques* in Quebec City. They're doing very well with government and the school boards," he said. "Maybe we can find a niche for STB with them. I hear what you're saying, Dale. It will certainly help, if we're better targeted and have a good sales presentation. I'll work up the pitch and a list of prospects with the sales team."

"Good, but first we need some input on the positioning from a technical standpoint," said Dale, turning to Guy, who still looked doubtful. "Guy, we need you to put together a competitive knock-off that shows how STB is better performance than any of the low-cost clones and better priced than ATI."

Guy frowned and slowly shook his head. "But Dale, we already know that it's not as good as the Graphics Solution, which is the closest equivalent from ATI. And STB is not always better performance than the imports, only more reliable, maybe."

Dale was suddenly agitated. "Christ Guy, this is a marketing and sales document I'm asking you for, not a technical report. Don't get too religious about it. You don't have to be *plus Catholique que le pape.* Even the Pope has to bend the facts a little to serve his higher purpose, now and then. We have to do the same to get our message out there and sell some product that doesn't drag us into the price wars. We have enough of that with the skinny margins on ATI."

He looked at the paperwork from STB on the conference table and pushed the marketing brochure and product specifications toward Guy. "We can only maintain our exclusivity with STB, if we meet the numbers I gave them. That's important to us, so give us what we need, please."

"OK, I'll see what I can do," Guy mumbled. "As long as it's still based on the facts." He got up and went back to his office in the service department.

Dale saw Patrick smile as Guy was getting the lecture, but he didn't want to acknowledge it and encourage the gloating. It was always a contest between the facts-oriented techies and the fast-talking sales prima donnas. Dale tried to get the best out of both sides and avoid too much scorekeeping over who was winning or losing. He went back to his desk and composed a fax to send to STB confirming the sales forecast.

7.

Back at home that evening, Dale's family was carrying on as usual in the few hours between school and suppertime.

"When is Daddy coming home?" asked Keira sticking her head around the corner into the kitchen.

"He'll be home soon, I think, sweetie," Susan replied. "He just likes to get a few things done at the office after everyone else has left."

"OK," said Keira, "I'm finished my homework for tomorrow. You want to shoot some hoops with me, Mommy?"

"No thanks sweetie. I'm making dinner and you know I'm terrible at basketball. Ask Sean if he's finished his homework."

"Nah, he's never interested. And he's even worse than you shooting hoops."

The Hunters lived in a spacious four-bedroom two-storey house in the comfortable upper-middle class suburb of the West Island of Montreal. They had purchased the house after Dale finished his studies at McGill and was starting work at AES Data. The future looked bright and they could finally afford to move out of their small apartment in the student ghetto near the university.

Neither Dale nor Susan were originally from Montreal. They were both small town kids from British Columbia and had met at the University of B.C. in Vancouver. They were married in Susan's home town of Nelson, B.C., before Dale came to McGill for his MBA. Sean was two and Susan was pregnant with Keira, when they moved into the house.

Susan had been concerned about their financial security when Dale lost his job at AES and then he ignored new job offers to start his own business, but she had confidence in him and supported his new venture.

Susan's parents were less confident and less supportive. They were California-born hippies and Susan's father was an anti-establishment American draft-dodger, who was outspokenly critical of "all those greedy capitalists who're just in it for the money." He didn't like to see his daughter join "that bunch of reckless, selfish bastards, screwing everybody just to make a buck."

Dale had turned it off long ago and stopped defending himself. Susan's parents would never be persuaded that not all entrepreneurs were evil. Dale was satisfied that they loved their daughter and their two grandchildren and otherwise accepted him as part of the family.

Keira went out the front door and Susan went back to the kitchen. She glanced at the digital clock on the back of the stove that read 6:35 and worried about Dale. *Why is he still at the office? He was out behaving badly with the visiting Texan last night. He said he'd be home for dinner tonight.*

I hope he's not getting into more trouble. This time the issues seem to be with Sammy in Boston. I still don't know what the hell is going on. It was dangerous and difficult enough to get away from the gangsters in Montreal, I hope he's not getting mixed up with Sammy and the gangsters in Taiwan now. From what I've read, these so-called Triads make the Montreal Mafia look like pussy cats.

Keira skipped down the front steps and over to the basketball net that was set up between the double garage doors. She picked up the basketball sitting in the rack at the bottom of the stand and dribbled in big bounces down the driveway, deking both ways around imaginary opponents, then turned and came back for a lay-up to hoist the ball with two hands up over her blond curls and banked it off the backboard into the net.

She exclaimed "Yes!" and did a major league fist-pump. Then spun around quickly and chased the ball down the driveway to pick it up before it rolled into the street. After retrieving it, she bounced it back towards the net to repeat the performance.

She didn't notice the dark blue sedan parked beside the curb a few houses down the street with a tall dark-skinned, greasy-haired man watching her closely through the tinted windshield.

****

"Something needs to change, Dale," said Susan. "I'm spending too much time worrying and I don't know what the hell's going on. I can see you're worrying, too, and you're not telling me anything."

They were sitting together in the family room. The TV was off and the kids had gone to bed. The house was quiet with lights off down the hall and in the living room. There was a glow into the front hallway from the counter top lights in the kitchen.

"What are you worrying about?" said Dale. "Everything's good. Just the usual business challenges trying to keep everything on track and avoid the obstacles. Sales are growing, profits are up and cash is flowing into our bank account. What've you got to worry about?"

"That's exactly what I'm worrying about. You not telling me the whole story. Not telling me what you're worrying about."

Dale slumped back into the easy chair facing Susan on the sofa. "I'm trying not to worry you about things you can't do anything about."

"I'm not saying I have the answers, Dale, but I deserve to know what's really going on. You need to share these things with me. That's what we need to do for a start."

"OK, I know. You're right. I love you, Susie. Sometimes, I try too hard to protect you and I get it wrong. Most of the business stuff, you don't need to know and I have lots of competent staff to deal with those issues. The only partner I have to manage now is Sammy Wong and he leaves me alone, pretty much. The distractions and the obstacles, well..." His voice trailed off, "Sometimes they're hard to avoid."

"Yes, I know the business is doing well and you're taking good care of it. It's the other stuff that makes me worry. What's Sammy got you into in Boston? And what about Gino Boncanno and his gang, what are they up to since they got shut down by Frank and his Mafia friends? Are we still in danger? What if Boncanno comes after us again?"

Dale avoided looking directly at Susan and leaned forward to put his elbows on his knees, his hands clasped together. *How much can I tell her? I need to keep her and the kids safe. It doesn't help to have her worrying, too. And I don't really have good answers, anyway.*

He looked up at her. "There's really nothing new to worry about, Susan. Sammy has me looking after a special shipment coming into Boston, but I'm keeping it all at arm's length and not doing anything wrong myself. For Boncanno, as far as I know, he's still shut down and out of business. He should never be back to bother us or anyone else. I've got Frank checking on him regularly and the Montreal Mafia are never going to let him get back into his old rackets again, so I think we're safe."

"I still worry."

"I'm sorry, but you wanted to know and that's all I've got. Sammy Wong's scheme should be a one-time thing and I don't think we have to worry about Boncanno."

"I hope you're right."

"So do I."

He sat forward and reached for the *TV Guide* magazine on the coffee table between them. "Now let's worry less and see if we can find a good movie to amuse ourselves."

Dale started browsing the pages for the evening's programming, but neither of them were focused on it.

Susan was staring at the blank screen, lost in thought.

"I don't think we should be so passive about it all," she said. "We seem to be just sitting and waiting for something bad to happen."

Dale looked back at her, wagging the remote control at the TV, without turning it back on.

"I'm not doing nothing, Susan. I'm trying to keep us safe, but I'm also trying to get the most out of the business, while we can. The opportunities won't last forever and it needs my full attention to avoid screwing it up. I just have to avoid the crooks and the bad ideas that get in my way."

"Maybe it's time to get out of the computer business. Sell it and start something else."

"That's the plan eventually, but not now. We're growing fast and building value in the business as it grows. I'm trying to make it as valuable as possible, but selling it and cashing out is still a few years away," said Dale.

"But you're taking a chance to get the timing exactly right. Isn't that a bad idea? Nobody knows when the good times will end. If you wait too long, everybody will be selling and nobody buying, right?"

"You're absolutely right and that's what I'm trying to avoid. You can be sure I'll do everything I can to find the right buyer and get the best price when I think the time is right, but it's not now."

"Fine, Dale, I understand that. But I still worry that all the pressures and the distractions will keep you from managing it to that happy conclusion. Why not accept what we've got and take our money out now. Then we can get out of harm's way and start something else, maybe even somewhere else. Why not retire young and do something completely different?"

Dale settled back in his chair and took the pose of 'The Thinker,' elbow on his knee, chin in his hand, scratching his head with the other hand. His seriousness was betrayed by the foolish grin that spread slowly across his face.

"Hey, I'm serious," said Susan. "How about getting into politics? You've always been interested in politics. You could run for Member of Parliament and do some good for the country, instead of being just another greedy, selfish entrepreneur trying to get rich and ignoring all the problems in the world around us. You know, the time might be right for you. Charles MacGregor, from down the street, came by this week looking for a donation to the Federal Liberal Party. He tells me that Mulroney is likely to call an election this fall and they need a good Liberal candidate in the riding. They're not very confident in their leader, John Turner."

"Oh, yeah. That's a great idea. Become a losing candidate for the Liberals in the next election. I don't have much confidence in Turner, either. He's a good man, but they're flogging the wrong horse with their anti-Free Trade rhetoric. I happen to agree with Mulroney that we'll be better off in a trade deal with the U.S. Maybe I should run for the Conservatives." He cocked his head and raised his palms, asking Susan to consider that idea.

She feigned an exaggerated look of disgust. "OK, forget it. Bad idea. Bloody Conservatives."

She reached for the remote and clicked the TV back on again.

"You really think I'm greedy and selfish?" Dale frowned and tried to look concerned. He didn't pull that off either.

Susan gave him a quick glance. "Just keep working hard, Dale, and get us off this merry-go-round you're on. The sooner the better. Then we can get on with the fun part of our lives, before we're too old to enjoy it."

8.

Dale had installed his New England office and warehouse space in an industrial park west of Boston, nestled among the glacier-polished granite boulders and tree-covered hillsides near Hopkinton, Massachusetts.

Hopkinton is best known as the starting point for the famous Boston Marathon. Every April, on Patriot's Day, thirty thousand runners start from Hopkinton and run the 26 miles, 42.2 kilometres, into downtown Boston. Dale was intrigued by his sudden proximity to the annual race and couldn't resist accepting the challenge to try it himself. *They're not all world class Olympic athletes. Lots of people, older and less fit than me, manage a marathon. Why not me?*

He trained for six months and then learned that he could not register for the Boston Marathon until he had run a prior marathon in less than three hours and fifteen minutes. He was disappointed not to be accepted, but then discovered there was a group known as 'The Outlaws,' who ran as unregistered runners at the back of the pack every year. Dale joined them for his first marathon and completed the endurance contest in a painful four-and-a-half hours. *I'm never doing that again. Why the hell would they put Heartbreak*

Hill in the middle of the race, just when our bodies are screaming at us to quit. Once is enough.

However, the bragging rights as a marathoner put him in an exclusive category of athletes, Olympian or not, and the ego appeal persuaded Dale to run three more marathons, two in Montreal and one in New York. Then he'd had enough, but decided to retain the bragging rights.

The facility for 3D Computer Products in New England was similar to the layout in Montreal with offices in front and a high-ceilinged warehouse and technical service area in back, but about one quarter of the size of the facilities in Montreal.

Dale was optimistic about growing the business quickly in New England and had taken an option on the unit next door, which would double the space available to him. He had already spoken to the developer in Boston to let him know that he expected to expand, as early as next year.

A blue-lettered sign in a metal frame on the brick wall above the front door identified the company.

3D-New England
Computer Display Products
Direct from the Manufacturer

Dale wanted to project an American image, as much as possible, so there was no indication of foreign ownership and no explanation that all the CHW computer monitors stacked high in the warehouse came from Sammy Wong's company in Taiwan, Chung-Wai.

There was also a requirement to hire American employees. During the first three months, Dale spent a lot of time there himself and used an agency for temporary staff until he was able to hire the initial complement.

His first hire was the Sales Manager, Shelly Carter. Shelly had several years of prior experience with some of the larger technology companies in the Boston area and she was keen to assume more responsibility in a smaller business.

The next recruits were Sandy Lyle for inside sales and customer service, Roberto Mancini, an electronics technician, and Helen Robertson for office administration. Sandy Lyle and Roberto Mancini were both versatile enough to assist with unloading the 40-foot containers arriving from Taiwan and to prepare the individual shipments for customers. The new staff at 3D – New England were all equally energetic and enthusiastic about contributing to the success of a small business in the fascinating and fast-changing new world of personal computers.

After a few months of training and supervision, Dale trusted them to manage on their own. Frequent phone calls were required back and forth to Montreal, but only occasional visits by Dale to New England.

Dale was following the same start-up business plan he had used in Montreal. His distribution business there now had grown to twenty-two employees and they were doing up to two million-a-month in sales during the best months, usually March for government year-end and September for back-to-school.

In New England, starting almost four years later, they were riding the back of the wave of personal computers washing across the country, hopefully not the tail-end or the receding tide. Business was tougher in New England against well-established competitors, who were not easily dislodged from the local computer retailers and systems builders by new suppliers like 3D Computers.

Customers took advantage of the competition and continually demanded lower prices and better terms. It was hard to grow revenues and maintain profitability with the continuing squeeze on profit margins.

Dale had the competitive advantage of receiving the CHW monitors at the lowest possible cost directly from the manufacturer, Chung-Wai. Sammy Wong was a supportive and equally ambitious partner in New England and he appreciated the financial performance that Dale was delivering to compensate for the poor results for CHW sales in California.

This evening, there was an empty container sitting on the truck trailer up against the closed doors at the warehouse loading dock waiting for the driver to come back and take it away in the morning. Dale was sitting inside the warehouse on a stool beside the service bench that Roberto Mancini used for testing and repair of monitors. He was looking at the small pile of six monitor cartons that he had separated from the rest and set against the wall. He stared at the yellow QA stickers signed by Sammy Wong on two sides of each box.

Dale had not yet made the phone call to the New York number that Sammy had given him. He was still wondering what was in the boxes and what he should do with them.

He turned to Frank the Fixer. "What do you think, Frank? Open them up and help ourselves. Tell these guys they got lost, somehow? Or just shut up and arrange to have them picked up?"

Frank had driven his Caddy down from Montreal the day before to meet Dale at the warehouse. He looked at Dale and raised his eyebrows. "You don't need me here, if you're just going to do as you're told. You want to make some trouble, right, Dale?"

"I just want to give these guys enough trouble they don't ask us to do it again."

"And what do you have in mind?"

"Well, I'm thinking we deliver the shipment as planned and prove we're good boys, doing as we're told. Then you show up and mess things up for them."

"OK, but where did I come from? How are they not going to connect me to you and Sammy Wong?"

"Yeah, that's the part I haven't figured out yet. You're supposed to be the creative one here. C'mon, Frank, be the Fixer."

"I think I need to know what we're working with. Let's open these boxes and find out what we've got."

"That's a good start, I agree. But let's wait until the end of the day and we can check 'em out when we're alone."

They were still sitting there and staring at the boxes, when Shelly Carter came into the warehouse looking for them.

"Hey Dale," she said, "You wanted us to start on this shipment with a new price list. Have you worked it up for us yet?"

"Yeah, Shelly. It's in my briefcase, I'll get it for you in the office." He stood and started back to the front offices.

Shelly lingered for a longer look at the handsome, wide-shouldered, young black man, before turning to follow Dale. Frank remained seated with his back to the service bench, facing the pile of six monitor cartons set against the wall. Shelly was curious about him, but they had not been introduced and she sensed that was not going to happen. Dale's friend seemed to be here on private business that Dale did not intend to share with his staff.

In a few minutes, Dale came back to the warehouse, meeting Shelly on the way. "The price list is on your desk, Shelly. Take a look and we can review it tomorrow morning."

Dale came back to the service bench and sat by Frank. They waited for the alarm system to beep a few minutes later, as the front door closed behind Shelly.

"OK, everybody's gone for the evening. Let's have a look at our special shipment," said Dale. He pulled one of the boxes closer to his stool and flipped it over to expose the taped bottom seam of the carton.

"Heavier than usual, so I'm thinking it's not another monitor." He sliced the tape with a yellow-handled Exacto knife and started to fold back the flaps. "I know it's supposedly been opened for QA inspection, but I'll re-tape it on the bottom, so it's not too obvious that we've had a second look."

Once the bottom flaps were opened and folded back, they pulled out the Styrofoam inserts that normally held a computer monitor firmly in place. In this box the standard inserts were intact, but there was no computer monitor inside. Instead, the monitor carton was full of smaller boxes packed tightly with popcorn foam filler that kept it all immoveable in the box. Dale removed one of the smaller boxes and opened it.

"Holy shit, these are CPU's."

He pulled out a cardboard insert from the small box. It had four computer chips about one-inch square, each sitting tightly under a blue antistatic plastic cover glued to the cardboard.

Dale showed Frank the black and purple-coloured box with an AMD logo and product data on the sides.

"These things are worth about eight hundred bucks apiece," said Dale. "That's thirty-two hundred per box and there must be... how many?"

"Interesting," said Frank. "I was expecting a box full of drugs, but this sounds even better. Now I understand the attraction of the computer business. High value in small packages. Just like drugs."

Dale ignored Frank's comparison to the drug trade and hoped that was never going to be part of Sammy's deals with the Triads. He stooped to reach inside the monitor carton and removed all of the small boxes, piling them on the service bench. He emptied the first open carton and counted them.

"Forty here, so that's about a hundred and twenty-eight thousand dollars' worth in one box. Compared to two hundred and sixty-seven dollars for the monitor that was removed."

"That sounds worth keeping for ourselves," said Frank.

Dale slumped back on the stool by the service bench and looked up at Frank. "I don't think I want anything to do with this shipment. No invoice, no paperwork at all, so it's definitely stolen product. That's what the Triads do and they're a pretty tough crowd, apparently. They help themselves to whatever they want, whenever they want it. Nobody holds out on the Triads. Sammy is under some heavy pressure to do what they asked for and he doesn't want me to do anything to piss them off."

"But you're going to take a chance on pissing them off, just a little, right?"

"Not me, you. I had nothing to do with it."

"Alright, we'll try that. It seems AMD is missing some product that's worth a lot more than your monitors. I'm sure I can find a buyer for it. Let's check out all six boxes, so we know what we've got."

They proceeded to open them all. It turned out that two of the boxes were full of CPUs and the four others were packed with two-hundred Micropolis 3-1/2-inch mini-floppy disc drives. They were the latest technology and currently in high demand and short supply, everywhere. Dale estimated those four boxes were worth another two hundred thousand.

"So we're sitting on about four hundred and sixty thousand in stolen product, hidden in my shipment. And it went through customs at a declared value of one hundred and twenty-three thousand. We're completely screwed, if this ever gets discovered."

"On the other hand," said Frank, "we could make a lot more money with this than you'll ever make selling your monitors."

"Well, you did say you'd like to try sales with 3D Computer Products. Let's see what you can do with our new product lines."

"No problem, I'll get right on it," said Frank. "But aren't you forgetting you already promised to deliver this stuff to somebody in New York?"

"Yeah, that's why I think we need this to be a two-step dance. First we deliver, then we steal it back. Or at least somebody mysteriously intercepts the run to New York and rips them off."

"Jesus, Dale, you're starting to sound like a criminal yourself."

"Yeah, that's your fault, leading me into a life of crime. But I'm counting on you to pull off the stealing part."

"I think I can find some friends to take care of that for you."

"OK, I think we have a plan. I'll make the delivery as promised. You set it up for these guys to get ripped off. I don't want to know who, how, or what happened. If you can make some money at it, go for it. Now you know what you're working with and how much it's worth."

"Yeah, this is gonna be great for me. How soon can you arrange the next shipment?"

"Go to Hell, Frank."

Dale clenched his fist in a gesture toward Frank's chin, then broke into a grin. Frank faked an exaggerated flinch from the threatened blow.

"This is supposed to end the arrangement for me, remember?" said Dale. "No more shipments of stolen product. I hope the Triads over there reach the same conclusion for Sammy, but I'm definitely staying away from any more of this smuggling part of his business. You can find yourself another partner, Frank, if you want to carry on from here. I'm out, when this is done."

"I'm not sure it'll be over that easy. Let's see how this works out for us. I'm sure we can find a way to make a little on this deal ourselves, but it'll be fun just to mess 'em up a little, anyway."

"You have a strange idea of what's fun, Frank. I doubt if they'll change their plans much, just because one shipment doesn't make it all the way home. There's lots more where that came from, I expect. And lots more eager buyers here, too. Business in stolen computer products will be good as long as the crooks can deliver when the suppliers can't. I know, it'd be better money than I can make in any legitimate business, but I'd still rather sleep soundly at night and be proud to tell my kids how I make a living."

"Jeez, Dale, you sound determined to be the last of the good boy scouts. Hope you make it, man. It'll renew my faith in humanity."

"Maybe you should try the straight and narrow yourself, Frank. Do you good to clean up your act and find a legitimate way to make a living. Forget the crooks and gangsters for a while. You must have some other useful skills you can sell."

"Nope, haven't found anything that works for me. I start flipping burgers or selling coffee and donuts, I'll end up killing somebody." He grimaced and thrust his big hands forward and held them out together like he was strangling somebody. "I like what I'm doing now. I'm just another humble entrepreneur trying to make a living. Like you Dale."

"Those two words, humble and entrepreneur, don't normally go together. Fortunately for you, because humble you're not."

Dale started stuffing the small cartons back into the monitor boxes the way he had found them. "That's enough of this bullshit for today, though. Let's go enjoy some good beer and seafood. That's the best part of doing business in Boston, the Sam Adams Boston Lager and the Legal Seafood restaurant. We can come back tomorrow to the dirty business of dealing in stolen goods."

He pushed the next box to Frank. "Here, you can help pack this up again. I won't send a fax to Sammy to let him know the shipment has arrived OK until you have a plan to take it from here. Then I'll make the call to New York for pickup when you're ready."

They locked up the office and warehouse and drove back to their hotel in the city. Dale in his blue BMW coupe and Frank in his black Caddy sedan.

*****

It was not Frank's first visit to Boston. He had friends there and he intended to speak to them about his need for some connections doing business in stolen product. He also had an introduction to some

Mafia friends in New York, who would appreciate the opportunity to pick up some high-value computer products.

Frank was thinking about his growing network among the Mafia families of Montreal and New York and his future opportunities.

You never know where these things might lead.

9.

The next day, Frank was on the phone to his contacts in Boston and New York.

He avoided too many details about the shipment from Taiwan, but let them all know that he had an opportunity to hijack some computer products. His friends were not quick to suggest anybody who could look after it for him.

He decided to get in touch with the contact in New York City he had been given by his Mafia connection in Montreal, Paolo Renaldi. Frank and Renaldi had worked on some mutually beneficial arrangements in the past, including helping Dale escape the clutches of Gino Boncanno. Renaldi ran a loan sharking and money laundering operation under the front of Ottimo Financial Services.

Renaldi had given Frank the name of Tony Di Staccato. Tony was the head of a criminal organisation that did business in New York and apparently had already been dealing in stolen computer products. Di Staccato had discovered it was a lucrative business that other gangsters and the biker gangs were ignoring and so were the cops. They were all paying more attention to the drug trade.

Di Staccato was generating quick cash from willing buyers on the black market and he had built a network for stolen product in New York, New Jersey, Atlanta and Miami. He had set up a legitimate business front, called Stack Distribution, with an office and warehouse in New Jersey. The computer business was useful for adding cash flow to his organisation and providing another outlet for money laundering. He had tried to introduce the Renaldi family to the computer business in Montreal, but they were not convinced it was worth the trouble in such a small market.

Di Staccato was enjoying a big cigar at home when he got the call from Frank. He sat deep in his plush armchair, blowing smoke rings at the stained glass lampshade that hung from the ceiling. He wore a black and gold-striped heavy satin bathrobe over a white T-shirt and boxer shorts. Tony was small in stature, but had a wide square face topped by a lush array of grey curls. His disproportionately large hands had fingers the same size as the thick round Cuban cigar he was holding. His skinny bare legs were crossed and he dangled a sheepskin-lined leather slipper from his toes.

"Sorry to call you at home, Mr. Di Staccato," said Frank, "But I got your name from my friend, Paulo Renaldi, in Montreal. He said you might be interested in some computer product I have in Boston."

"OK, Frank. Paulo knows me well enough not to waste my time, but I don't like to do business over the phone at home. Can I call you back from another phone, tomorrow?" Di Staccato's thick black eyebrows danced above his steel rimmed glasses like animated exclamation marks as he spoke.

Frank explained to Tony that it was urgent, because the shipment was in transit and he needed to make arrangements to intercept it soon, before it left Boston and he lost track of it.

"Could you call me back at my hotel tonight from another phone?" Frank gave him the hotel phone number and his room number with the name he had used at check-in, Frank Abbott.

The desk clerk hadn't asked for ID and Frank preferred to avoid the confusion of trying to spell out Faysal Mohamed Abou, which too often led to more quizzical looks and inquiries into his identity. Better to let them think he was African American. Frank Abbott would do.

Di Staccato agreed to call Frank back. He went out to the kitchen where two men were sitting playing cards. They sat at the centre-island kitchen counter in open-neck white shirts with their ties pulled loose and their shirt cuffs rolled up. Their suit jackets hung on a coat rack beside the back door. The older man was small and wiry with grey hair, the younger one was an overweight forty year-old with broad shoulders and heavy arms filling his shirt sleeves. Each man had a gun lying on the countertop beside the crib board and within easy reach as they played their hands.

Within half an hour, Frank got a call at the hotel. The older man from Tony's kitchen was calling from a pay phone. He didn't sound pleased to have had his card game interrupted.

"Stack asked me to call you. You have some product for us?"

"Yeah, I have about five hundred thousand dollars' worth of computer CPU chips and micro disc drives. They're sitting in a warehouse here, near Boston. I'd like to find a good home for it all, before it goes to somebody else.

"We might be interested, if the price is right. How much are you asking for it?"

"Actually, the product is no charge. But there's a catch."

"There's always a goddamn catch. What is it this time?"

"You'll have to steal it from the people who are coming to pick it up tomorrow. We want to deliver it to them and let them leave happy, then we need you guys to take it off their hands."

"That's a strange arrangement, why do you want to make it so goddamn complicated, if you already have the goods in Boston?"

"Well, here's the story. My friend, with the computer distribution business here, received the goods hidden in a shipment from his supplier in Taiwan. He doesn't want anything to do with it. He would like to be sure it doesn't happen again by making sure it gets screwed up on delivery. Actually, after delivery is better, like I just said, so we can't be accused of deliberately sabotaging the deal."

"And you want us to do that. Gimme a minute."

He paused and it sounded like he had covered the telephone mouthpiece, as he spoke to someone else before coming back on the line.

"It sounds like the goddamn Chinese Triads are involved, probably at both ends."

"You're probably right. Is that a problem?"

"Hell no. They don't scare us. Makes it more interesting. We can screw them up and push 'em out of business at the same time. But why are you doing all this for nothing?"

"Well, first I'm trying to get my friend out of the business of smuggling stolen product. He has this strange obsession with trying to make money the hard way. Second, I'm trying to make a good impression on Mr. Di Staccato. He seems like a good guy to know and I'm always looking for work. I'm not like my friend here, I don't mind taking some risks and getting my hands dirty. You can check me out with the Renaldis in Montreal. Tell Tony I'll accept whatever he thinks is a reasonable finder's fee for this job. I wouldn't want him to get the idea I work for nothing."

"I see." There was another brief pause, then he said, "OK, I think we can make a deal on those terms. What do you need from us?"

"I need you to meet me here with one or two other cars, so we can arrange a tag team to follow the guys who come to do the pick-up. We don't know where they're going and maybe you'll want to hijack them en route. Maybe follow them back to wherever. It would help if your guys are equipped with mobile phones."

"Got it, no problem. Somebody else will call you at the hotel tonight and you can arrange to meet up with them. You'll hear from a guy named Carlo."

OK, we have a plan, thought Frank, as he placed the hotel phone back on the night stand and lay back on the bed.

What could possibly go wrong?

10.

It was late on Thursday afternoon two days later and Dale was alone in the warehouse at 3D – New England waiting for pickup of the special delivery from Sammy Wong.

He had made the call that morning to the number Sammy had given him. The six boxes were now sitting near the loading dock at the back of the warehouse. They still had the yellow QA stickers on them and there were no noticeable indications that they had been opened or tampered with.

Dale was holding his best poker face to avoid showing any nervousness about the shipment. He heard a vehicle pull up outside followed by a buzz at the side door entrance.

He opened the door to a skinny Chinese man standing on the outside landing. Another man, same build, but taller and wearing sunglasses, stood by the open rear doors of a white minivan.

"You called about six cartons you have for us?"

Yeah, pleased to meet you. No name, no paperwork. Not the way I normally do business, but fine by me. This is not normal business and I don't want to know any more than I do already. Nothing to tell, if anybody ever asks.

"Here you go," said Dale, pushing the boxes to the loading dock. He hit the switch to raise the wide warehouse door towards the ceiling.

The taller man outside stepped forward and started pulling the boxes off the dock to load the van. The other one went back down the steps to help him push all six into the back.

They slammed the rear doors shut and got back into the front seats without a word or gesture. The minivan pulled away to go around the building and back out to the front street.

Delivery's done, I'm out of here. They're all yours now, Frank.

Dale rushed inside and sat in a back office to call Frank's mobile phone in the Caddy. He was supposed to be waiting with an eye on the lane from the rear of the warehouse to the street.

"You got 'em?" he said, when Frank picked up. "They're in the rusty white van, says Long Island Electric on the side, I think."

"Yeah, no problem. We're on it."

"OK. Have a nice trip to New York. You can tell me all about it when I see you again. Hope your plan works out. I'm heading home."

"It never goes entirely according to plan, but we'll work it out. See you in Montreal."

Dale gathered up his papers and briefcase, turned out the lights and set the alarm as he was leaving.

He climbed into his BMW-M3 and headed for the Mass Pike and Highway 95 North back to Montreal. He had made the trip many times, back and forth over the U.S. border between Quebec and Vermont to 3D – New England in Massachusetts. One friendly

Customs and Immigration Agent at the U.S. border crossing coached Dale never to say he was going there to work.

"Mr. Hunter, you're just going to check on your business investment, right? You don't have a visa to work in the U.S., so you've hired only legal American citizens to work there, right? You're just goin' to see how they're doin.' Right?"

"Yeah, that's exactly right," said Dale. He was more careful in his choice of words from that point on, to avoid the risk of being flagged as an illegal visitor and taking a lot more than the usual 30-second stop on entry to the U.S.

The drive through Vermont, in either direction, was always a pleasure on the smooth winding roads curving along the hillsides, unless winter conditions made it hazardous. Focusing on the road and enjoying the scenery enabled Dale to decompress from the usual stress of managing his business. After this trip to New England managing Sammy Wong's special delivery, he was in particular need of calming BMW-therapy through the mountains.

High-speed driving seemed to be acceptable in Vermont, judging by the local green licence plates that Dale followed at speeds well over the 60 mile-per-hour posted speed limit. The broad divided highway allowed him to let his eyes wander over the green hills and appreciate the scenery even at high speed. *Les verts monts*, named by the original French-Canadian explorers, the green mountains.

Just hills, really, thought Dale. *There aren't any real mountains east of the Rockies. The first Europeans to see them were the French-Canadian explorers, De La Verendry et fils, the father and his four sons. Les Rocheuses, they called them. They also explored all the way from Montreal down the Mississippi and built the original settlement of Nouvelles Orléans.*

Dale smiled at the way people now pronounced New Orleans and other French-named cities, like Detroit and Des Moines. Far removed from the Old French of Normandy in France, where many of the first colonists in Canada came from and which was the origin of the French dialect still spoken in Quebec. Dale had great difficulty with it when he first arrived in Montreal, because it was so different from the international French he had learned at high school in B.C.

Americans tended to forget the French explored their country long before the English colonists pushed west from New England and the Carolinas. Most of the south and central States along the Mississippi remained French territory until Napoleon sold it all to President Jefferson in the Louisiana Purchase of 1805. He needed the money to fight the English back in Europe. The people of French origin and the place names remained. The Cajuns of Louisiana were originally the Acadians from New Brunswick, who had been forcibly removed by the British in fear of potential revolt by Canadian supporters of the American War of Independence.

Dale was reflecting on the long shared history of Americans and Canadians under British and French colonial rule, before they achieved independence for their own nations.

"Ah, shit!" He cursed out loud, as he saw the flashing red and blue lights of a Vermont State Trooper in his rear-view mirror.

He lifted his foot off the gas and watched the speedometer needle slip below 130 kilometres-per-hour. The cop must have caught him on radar doing over ninety miles-an-hour. Dale pulled over and stopped on the shoulder of the highway. He opened the driver's side window and waited for the officer to approach his car.

"Enjoying the good roads here, sir? I know you can't drive that fast in Quebec, your roads are terrible."

Dale reached for his driver's licence and car registration, which he handed out the window. "Yeah, you're right. Sorry about that, Officer."

"Sorry about the bad roads in Quebec? I'm sure it's not your fault. But it would make my annual fishing trip a lot easier if you could fix 'em up a little." He smiled and peered past Dale to look around inside the car. "I clocked you doing ninety-seven miles-an-hour back there, sir."

He held Dale's driver's licence against the large pad in his hand and copied the information onto the ticket he was writing.

"That's not a good speed to hit a moose," he said.

"Yeah, I know. I thought I was just keeping up with the locals. I didn't notice I was going so fast after they pulled off, I guess."

"Well, the locals know where to slow down. You should pay more attention, Mr. Hunter. I'll put you down at eighty-five to save you a few bucks. Don't forget to mail it back in U.S. dollars. If it's not paid and we pull you over again, it'll be outa the car and straight to jail."

He tore off the ticket and handed it through the window to Dale. "Here you go. Drive safe now."

Back on the road, Dale drove slower and kept his high beams on as much as possible to scan the woods on both sides of the road and look for any moose stepping out.

He was thinking he should call Susan and let her know when to expect him home. Before he could reach for the handset snapped into the holder beside him, the key pad lit up and the phone rang. He tapped the call button and spoke towards the mic clipped onto the sun visor above his line of sight.

"Hello?"

He heard Frank's voice. "Hey, Dale. You still on the road, too?"

"Yeah, about two hours from home. Where are you?"

"We're still following your shipment in the van. I've got two other cars with me and they're equipped with mobile phones, too. My new friends from New York are very modern and up to date with technology. Must be because they're in the computer business, like you."

"Yeah, we're all so friggin' modern these days. I'm surprised the reception is this good in the mountains of Vermont. You're saying the van is still on the road since they picked up and left the warehouse?"

"Yup, we're still going south on I-95, nearly at New York City. We decided to follow them to their destination, instead of running them off the road for only six boxes of product. There's probably more to pick up where they're going. I'll call you tomorrow for an update."

"That's not necessary, Frank. I don't need to know more. Now let me call my wife and let her know I'm on the way and I managed to avoid all the shit you'd like to get me into."

"Jeez, Dale, you're missing all the fun. See you in Montreal."

They hung up and Dale stared ahead as his headlights washed the darkness away from the highway.

Good luck to you, Frank, but that's not the kind of fun I'm looking for. Susan's still worrying about the last time we were dragged into this stuff. We've both had enough of it.

His speed increased, as did the worries about his family back home.

11.

Frank's tag team had followed the white van from the 3D – New England warehouse out to the highway and the toll booths to the 495 Freeway, then they headed south until it merged with the Interstate highway I-95. They continued south toward New York City and after three-and-a-half hours on the road with only one quick stop for gas, coffee and a restroom break, they followed the van past the exits leading into New York and continued on the New Jersey Turnpike leading toward Newark and Jersey City.

The week-day traffic remained heavy all the way. Long distance 18-wheelers stretched out among all the other vehicles moving at speed. With everyone cautiously weaving from lane to lane, the three pursuing vehicles were able to blend in while keeping the van in sight. Frank used the mobile phone in his Caddy to keep in touch with the two other drivers to rotate the vehicle that followed closest behind the van.

In Jersey City, the van left the freeway and Frank's crew cautiously followed it into a rundown industrial area, not far from the Hudson River. The bright lights of Manhattan were visible across the river. The three drivers did not dwell on the skyline as the van pulled into a large parking lot surrounded by a chain-link fence. The van drove straight ahead across the gravel-surfaced lot to a grey galvanized metal building with faded blue and red lettering on a large sign at the top that read, The Federal Box Company, and stopped in front of the wide garage doors. Frank heard it honk twice and the doors rolled open. The van drove in and the two Chinese men stepped out of it as the doors closed behind them.

Frank made a mental note of the street signs at the corner where he had stopped in his Caddy, indicating 23rd Avenue East and Horton Street. The three vehicles were all parked at a discrete distance from the Federal Box Company building, but Tony Di Staccato's two men could still watch the warehouse entrance. They watched the building together for almost an hour, before Frank decided to leave them to continue their surveillance without him.

"They're all yours now," Frank said over the car phone to Carlo. "You guys have everything you need to do whatever you want. Let Tony know I'll call him later this evening after I get settled into my hotel." He left the industrial sprawl of New Jersey and drove back into New York City.

Before leaving Montreal three days earlier, Frank had called his cousin in New York and asked him to reserve a good hotel. The reservation was at the Burton Suites, not far from Central Park. Frank found it and managed to fit the Caddy into a cramped underground parking lot across the street which was going to cost almost as much as a good hotel in Montreal, he thought. He was satisfied with the choice, however, after settling into his comfortable old-fashioned hotel room.

He made the call to Tony Di Staccato, who sounded pleased with the results of the day and was insistent that Frank come over to his place for a late dinner. It was not far away from the Burton Suites on the other side of Central Park in the Upper East Side. "I'd like to see you, kid. I talked to Paulo Renaldi and he thinks we should meet. You never know, we might do business again someday."

Frank was quick to accept and smiled as he opened his bag on the bed. *Just what I was thinking. Thanks, Paulo, I'm sure Tony has lots going on that I can help him with and he's probably more generous than the Renaldi family.*

After a quick shower and change into a white silk shirt and fresh blue jeans, Frank took the short taxi ride over to Di Staccato's address. It was a stylish luxury New York 1920s-era apartment building. The uniformed doorman walked Frank to the elevator and hit the button for the ninth floor.

"Mr. Di Staccato is number nine-o-two," he said.

A few minutes later, Frank was sitting comfortably at the centre island in the kitchen of Tony "Stack" Di Staccato. Tony was hovering over the big black gas-fired stove, dicing peppers, mushrooms and onions and tossing them into a stainless steel pot of bubbling tomato sauce, beside a large cauldron of water coming to a boil. Beside the stove was a flat box of linguini.

"So, where you from, kid," said Tony, looking at the young man helping himself to another strip of prosciutto and a slice of parmigiana that he placed beside the olive bread on his plate.

Frank raised his glass of red wine in a toast and smiled. "This is all very good, Tony. Thank you."

He sipped the wine and said, "To answer your question, *je suis un Québecois de la belle ville de Montréal.* I'm a Quebecer from the beautiful city of Montreal."

"Yeah, OK, so you speak French, too. But I don't mean since yesterday. What I mean is where from, originally?"

"Ah, originally I'm from Mogadishu, Somalia. That's in the northeast, what they call the Horn of Africa. I came to Canada from there about eleven years ago."

"African, huh. Why didn't you come to America? We got lots of Africans here."

"I guess somebody decided you didn't need any more Africans. And I'm not sure we're all that well treated in America, either. Canada was easier and seemed like a good idea. Montreal's been good to me."

Tony nodded and continued stirring the tomato sauce, releasing more delightful aromas into the air.

"I hear you've been helpful to the Renaldis and they tell me I can trust you, Frank. So it seems your little trip to Jersey might work out very well for everybody. I figure there's more in that warehouse than your six boxes. We're going in tomorrow night to take it all off their hands. Maybe you want to help us finish the job. We won't be long, but we don't plan to leave anybody in business there after we're done. Is that the message you want to send back to Taiwan?"

"Yeah, that sounds about right. If you can shut them down, their connections in Taiwan might leave my friend's partner there alone, too. Help yourself to anything you want in their warehouse. I'm sure it'll be worth your while, but you don't need my help. Your guys seem to know what they're doing. I'm sure they can handle any resistance that might come up."

"You're right, they'll manage. Your work is done here," said Tony.

He turned to the counter beside the stove and pulled open a drawer. Frank saw a handgun and some bundles of cash tucked into the drawer. Tony pulled out an envelope and tossed it across the counter to him. "I appreciate the opportunity you brought us, Frank, so here's ten-grand for your trouble."

Frank looked at the envelope, then up at Tony.

"I was thinking twenty-five would be about right."

Tony's head jerked up with a start. He glanced at the big stainless cauldron that was now boiling with the steam rising into the fume hood above it, then turned to Frank.

"You got balls, kid. I invite you into my home and now you want to hold me up? I thought you didn't want to be paid at all, you just wanted the introduction."

"Well, that's right, I did say that, but I was told you were a reasonable man and I thought twenty-five thousand would be a reasonable fee for my efforts. As you just said, you'll probably pick up a lot more than we delivered to you and that was worth half a million by itself. I'm not looking for any gifts, Tony, I'm just trying to establish a good business-like relationship. Maybe I can do more for you another day."

Tony pursed his lips and exhaled looking straight into the dark eyes of Frank the Fixer. He shook his head slowly and turned back to the drawer.

Frank watched him closely. *Jesus, I hope he doesn't pull out the gun. We don't want blood mixed with the tomato sauce in his kitchen.*

Tony pulled out a wrapped bundle of cash and tossed it on top of the envelope.

"OK, another ten grand makes twenty. Now I have a hard-ass Somalian on the payroll."

He threw his head back and laughed loudly, then reached across the counter and gripped Frank's hand in a firm shake. He turned to the stove and pulled the box of linguini forward, grabbing a handful and placing it carefully into the pot of bubbling hot water. "Now, let me show you some good New York Italian cooking. Not like that pale imitation you got in Montreal."

"It all tastes good to me," said Frank. *And I'm happy to extend my Mafia dining network from Montreal to New York. I wonder who I'll be calling on next.*

12.

After the evening with Tony Di Staccato, Frank had decided to stay in New York for another day. They had agreed to meet again on Sunday, before Frank drove back to Montreal. He was enjoying the comfortable hotel and a run in Central Park on Saturday morning appealed to him.

He left the hotel in shorts and a tee-shirt and weaved carefully through the pedestrians on the sidewalk for a few blocks, then jogged into the park through the entrance off Park Avenue and picked up his stride.

The park was occupied, but not busy, as he loped along the paved trails that wound below the grassy slopes and across the playing fields. It felt good to be exerting himself and he sped up on the long straight path across an open field. Half way across, he noticed a green tennis ball rolling across the grass toward him, just as a big bounding dog raced up and clamped its jaws on the ball. The dog looked like a Boxer, with its stocky build and square face, short tawny hair and white markings. The dog was startled by the man who was running away quickly and suddenly dropped the ball, growled and raced after Frank, barking fiercely.

A hefty blonde woman in black tights and a billowing green sweat shirt, waved her leash after them, screaming, "Bingo, no. Bingo! Come back! Bingo!"

Frank looked back at the onrushing dog. He stopped and turned to face it head-on, crouched in a fighting stance. The dog skidded to a halt, continuing to snarl at Frank. They looked at each other warily, waiting for the next move.

Frank slowly raised his left hand above his head and watched the dog's eyes follow it upwards. He lunged forward, caught the dog's collar in his right hand, twisted it hard and yanked the dog vertically to his chest with its front legs pinned under his left arm.

The dog's hind legs flailed and its breathing got weaker. Frank held the wheezing bundle tightly and strode toward the blonde woman standing wide-eyed on the path beside a park bench. Frank stood in front of her and gradually released the dog's collar. As the dog relaxed in his arms, Frank whispered in its ear.

"Hey buddy, settle down and we can be friends. Let me give you back to mommy."

He dropped the dog at the woman's feet. The Boxer coughed and scrambled behind her to get beneath the park bench. The woman looked at Frank and swallowed hard.

"Sorry," she said, before kneeling down and clipping the leash to its collar.

Frank turned and jogged back to the paved path. *Maybe the stupid bitch will learn to keep away from joggers in the park.* He wasn't thinking of the dog.

After Frank's run, he went back to the hotel and pumped iron for almost an hour in the gym. Back in his room after a long hot shower and wrapped in a large white towel, he sat on the bed and dialed the phone to call Montreal. A man answered.

"*La Police de la ville de Montréal, Station vingt-et-un,* MUC Montreal Police, Station Twenty-one. *Bonjour,* may I help you?"

Frank asked for Detective Hélène Bourassa, who should be working on her paperwork at that hour. The call was transferred to her desk where she picked it up.

"Hey, beautiful, you're looking good this morning."

"Hi, Frank, thanks. I am looking particularly good this morning. How about you? Taking care of yourself in New York?"

Frank and Hélène occasionally worked together as Frank was good at pushing beyond the legal boundaries and Hélène appreciated his ability to find pieces of the puzzle that she could not. They kept their personal relationship discreet, as her superiors were suspicious that Frank was working more often with the criminals than he was with the police.

"I'm just getting warmed up in New York," said Frank, "but so far, so good. You should be here, too, Hélène. We could have some fun Saturday night in New York, don't you think?"

"Thanks, Frank, but I'm busy here spoiling Saturday night for some of your old friends in Montreal. So I've got work to do, no time for chit-chat."

"OK, go ahead. I'm making some new friends here and they're going to be spoiling the fun for somebody tonight, too. I'm going to have a quiet evening visiting my cousins from Somalia that I haven't seen for a couple of years."

"You don't need any more dangerous friends, Frank. It's a much better idea for you to spend time with your family and try behaving for a change."

"Behaving is boring. And the dangerous friends pay good money. More dangerous, more money. I already earned a little bonus I can spend on you when I'm home, Hélène. Don't knock it."

"OK, Frank, but I don't want to know too much about the deals you make. Keep it quiet and take care of yourself."

"I always do. Probably not home until late tomorrow night, so I'll call you Monday."

Even after the jog and the phone call, Frank arrived at the dining room before nine for a breakfast of eggs benedict with smoked salmon on a New York bagel. *Dale would be complaining that a New York bagel isn't as good as a Montreal bagel. But he's not here and I'm loving New York.*

After breakfast Frank got back on the phone and did the rounds of people he knew in the city. He confirmed dinner plans with his cousin and which subways to take out to their place in Brooklyn. He spent the afternoon walking the streets of Broadway and Times Square and observing the sights of Manhattan. *This place is unique in the world and about as far as I could possibly get from Mogadishu. Huge and very impressive. New York makes even Montreal look like a poor village in the country.*

With his cousin, they talked of Somalia and their families back home, but Frank's mind was on the likely scenarios in New Jersey, where Tony Staccato's men were going after the stolen product and putting the local Triad connection out of business.

*****

Frank and Di Staccato had agreed to meet again at the offices of Stack Distribution in New Jersey, so Frank packed up and moved out of the hotel after breakfast on Sunday. He drove through the Holland Tunnel to Interstate 95 and over to Newark. The Stack Distribution offices and warehouse were not far off the highway.

He parked the Caddy in front, well away from the entrance, and took a long walk toward the front doors, so they could see him coming. He held his arms wide and palms up. Inside the front door, two heavies overwhelmed a small desk in front of the stairs leading up to the mezzanine level above the warehouse floor.

Frank came in the door and stopped in front of the desk. The two men, now both standing, looked at the wide-shouldered young black man, taller than both of them.

He said, "I'm Frank. Tony's expecting me."

One muscle-bound heavy patted him down, while the other kept his hand on the gun holster at his belt. Muscle-bound said, "Upstairs, on the right."

Frank went up to the mezzanine and looked out over the warehouse with boxes stacked in piles over the floor. He looked quickly for the six CHW monitor boxes, but didn't see them. He turned right toward a closed door, opened it and stepped into the large office.

Tony Di Staccato was seated in a straight-backed wooden chair in front of a wide metal desk. Sitting behind the desk was a middle aged man in a blue silk shirt, who rose to greet Frank. Against the wall to the left were two more heavy-set men in suits sitting beside a small table, facing Tony. Tony got up and shook Frank's hand.

"Hello, Frank. This is Pat Cametti. He runs our computer business." He indicated the smartly dressed man at the desk. "He's the only one around here, who knows anything about all this high technology crap we're moving."

Tony ignored the two men against the wall. Cametti reached across the desk to shake Frank's hand.

"What's your last name, by the way, Frank?" asked Tony.

"Well, my real name is not Frank at all, it's Faysal. For Somalians, my name is Faysal Mohamed Abou. Not so easy to say, or to spell or remember, for most folks over here. So in Montreal, they know me best as Frank. Frank the Fixer, actually."

Tony smiled and shrugged. "Somalian tough guy, like I told you," he said to Cametti.

"Pleased to meet you, Frank," said Cametti. "Seems we could do business together. I'm wondering if you can get us some more of the same products."

"Last night's little pickup was very good for us," added Tony. "Your six boxes, plus some other high value merchandise. Shutting down the competition was a bonus."

Frank nodded. "Glad it all went so well."

"Not so well for them," said Tony. "They lost all that product and a few of their guys, too."

He grinned at Pat Cametti, then turned back to Frank. "We have a proposal for you and your friends. You were telling me, Frank, this shipment was buried in a container from Taiwan with a delivery to your warehouse in Boston, right? Well, we'd like to do a few more shipments like that, but without the detour to the guys in Jersey City. We won't need to go to all that trouble next time." He grinned again.

Frank rubbed the scar on the left side of his jaw. "Well, all that sounds interesting, but there's a problem. My friend in Boston and his supplier in Taiwan are both reluctant to deal in stolen product. They want this to end. Not to continue."

Tony shrugged again. "I'm sure they can be persuaded. We'll make it worth their while and it'll be mostly legit. I'll put a couple hundred grand up front for the product, any time they're ready to deliver. Pat has a list of products in big demand right now. He can get us top dollar. We'll pay you and your buddies well, too. We're not greedy and we look after our partners."

He paused and watched for Frank's reaction. There was none, so he continued.

"Take our shopping list to your guys and see what you can do for us, Frank. You're already on the payroll, remember. Time for Frank the Fixer to get to work."

Frank rubbed the scar on his jaw again. "OK, it's worth a shot. I'll get back to you next week. We'll try to find a way to make it happen and keep everybody happy with their piece of the action."

Frank stood and shook hands with Tony and Pat Cametti, then headed for the door. They all continued to ignore the two silent heavies sitting against the wall.

*****

OLD TIMERS & HOCKEY MEMORIES

"We really are a pathetic pair of cranky old farts," said Dale.

"Speak for yourself," said Frank, "I'm not nearly as old as you and definitely not as cranky."

They were sitting on bar stools at the Bell Centre, home arena of the Montreal Canadiens NHL hockey team since 1996. They had just been in the arena to watch an early season game.

"Sounded like you were bitching about being old and bored, like me," said Dale.

"I was only bitching about the boring hockey game," said Frank. "The Canadiens used to be a lot more fun to watch. Remember back in the 80s when they were battling the Québec Nordiques?" Frank shook his head and drained his beer glass. "Who the hell cares about the Canadiens playing a hockey team from Nashville, Tennessee?"

"Actually, Nashville is worth watching with P.K. Subban playing," said Dale. "He's always exciting and still working hard to prove the Canadiens were wrong with their dumb-ass move, trading him to Nashville, a couple of years ago. Useless coaches couldn't manage their most talented player. Sure, he has a big personality and gets too much attention, but if he's attracting fans and taking the team deep into the playoffs, so what? They couldn't handle him, so they sent him packing. Management's the problem, not P.K. Subban." As an old entrepreneur, Dale thought he knew bad management when he saw it. He continued his rant.

"There's a prima donna on every winning team. What the hell were they thinking? He's delivering results and they decide to fire him and keep the useless complainers who are not performing? Unbelievable incompetence, if you ask me."

"I didn't ask, but thanks for the lecture, Dale. Anyway, I like P.K. Subban, too," said Frank. "Not because he's black and probably fighting blatant racism everywhere he goes, but he's talented and obviously loves the game. Sure, he sucks up a lot of air time, but I agree he's exciting to watch. Worth the price of admission like Guy Lafleur used to be."

"Right. Lafleur could be a problem too. They managed to keep him in the line-up and win a few Stanley Cup Championships even." Dale shrugged. "But what the hell do we know? These managers and coaches are still getting the big bucks, so they must be getting the job done, as far as the owners are concerned, anyway."

"Yup, we're just two more ignorant fans," said Frank, "Ranting about bad management and missing the good old days. Grouchy old men, like you said."

They did not appear that decrepit. Dale was still slim and fit with only a few wrinkles and sags that he had acquired over the past thirty years. His formerly dark hair had thinned and gone grey at the temples and his moustache was now sprinkled with salt and pepper. He projected a youthful energy that denied his sixty-plus years.

Frank was almost ten years younger and he still had a solid frame several inches taller than Dale. The slight paunch above his belt didn't make him look any less physically imposing.

They swirled the beer in the bottom of their glasses. They had been reminiscing about the good old days and their thoughts turned inevitably to their adventures together fighting criminals and the threats of violence and murder. They were both lost in thought. Frank was first to return to the present.

"So, let's get back to managing our own lives instead of bitching about everybody else's. More excitement would be good for you, don't you think, Dale."

"Nope, I'm content to relax and reminisce about the good old days. I'm busy enough enjoying my retirement."

"Wow, sounds like you are getting old, man. Not me," said Frank, shaking his head vigorously, "I'm still getting lots of excitement. More than I can handle, sometimes."

"You're such a bull-shitter."

"No bullshit." Frank laughed. "It's too hard to get you excited, though. I'm ready to give up on you. But what about the old crime fighting days? That was fun. You enjoyed the excitement then, didn't you?"

"Absolutely not. Are you trying to spoil the evening entirely? Those days are not among the good memories. Jesus, Frank, now I need another beer." Dale scowled and looked for the bartender to signal a request for two more beer, then he reached for a menu and flipped it open. "Let's have a look at something to eat. I'm not in the mood for cooking tonight and I know you never bother."

"I wouldn't say never," replied Frank. "But there are so many great restaurants in Montreal, how can I compete? You want to try my new favourite Italian spot tonight? It's on me, since you looked after the hockey and the beer."

"Well, I'm not so sure about joining you and your Italian friends. They haven't always been so good for my health and I'm not talking about the food."

He put down the menu and looked to Frank for a response. The bartender set down two more draft beer on the bar in front of them and left with the two empty glasses.

"C'mon, Dale," said Frank, "time to get past the old stereotypes. You're still stuck in the 80s. Doesn't matter where they come from, there's always a few bad bastards out there. You've met a few bad Italians, but most are pretty ordinary, just trying to make an honest living, like you and me. You've gotta learn to forgive and forget."

"Well there's a few, like Gino Boncanno, I'll never forgive or forget," said Dale. "But I'll try to be more open-minded about Italians, just for you." He raised his glass toward Frank and Frank lifted his in return.

Dale said, "So, enough moaning and bitching about hockey and our criminal past. Let's go for dinner. Glad to hear you're buying for a change and not giving me that old act about being a poor Somalian immigrant."

"Hey, another bad stereotype. Don't worry, I've got his one. Forget Italian, let's go to the *Baton Rouge*. It's always good."

"Good choice. It'll be a nice change from hot dogs and beer. Quick, before you change your mind."

=====

Part 2:

It's Never that Simple

13.

Dale and Frank often met in their cars, either Frank's black Caddy sedan or Dale's blue BMW-M3 coupe. Frank's big frame fit better in the Caddy, but Dale loved any excuse to show off his sporty BMW.

That afternoon in Montreal, they were parked in the Caddy at the back corner of the lot at Lafleur's hot dog stand, trying to avoid spilling mustard, relish or ketchup on Frank's black leather seats.

"Maybe you could take me to some of Montreal's fine dining spots for a change, Dale. It's time we stopped meeting in my car."

"We could use mine," said Dale, "but you prefer to spread out in the Caddy."

"You're sporty little Bimmer isn't built for giants from Africa."

"Oh, I'm sure BMW could find something that you'll fit in, If you really want to upgrade from this big American cruise ship. Young guy like you, you should get a car that's built for driving, not cruising."

"Careful, buddy, you wanna walk back to the office?"

"No, thanks. You can turn up the AC a little, though. I'm not sure if it's the hot, humid weather or your really dumb idea that's making me sweat."

Dale was listening to the new proposition that Frank had brought back from New York. He wasn't buying it.

"What the hell are you thinking, Frank? Now you want me to get in bed with the New York Mafia? You were supposed to end it in New York, not sign us up for more."

"Look Dale, let's not worry too much how other people do business. Think of it as just another customer and an opportunity to make a few bucks."

"I'm always in favor of making a few bucks and I know opportunities can disappear real quick, regardless of where they come from. But there are two problems here. First, we have to get Sammy onside to supply the goods. I know he still has to work with the Triads, but I'm not sure he wants to get in deeper by asking them to supply more product. Second, I don't want to get more involved in this illegal shit, myself. I want to be kept as far away from it as possible."

"Understood, Dale. But you know you're probably already selling to people who buy stolen goods anyway, right? That's how you got introduced to Gino Boncanno in the first place, remember? He was selling stolen product to your customer, André Lebeau, at Lebeau's computer store downtown, *InfoCité*."

Dale was shaking his head. "Yeah, I remember. That was how the nightmare started and I'm not so sure it's over yet with Boncanno."

"It won't be over 'til Gino's dead. He can't be scared off forever, Dale. He's likely going to come after you again at some point. But let's leave that sleeping dog alone for now and work with these guys in

New York. They want to do business with us, so let's grab it while we can. You and Sammy can even find a way to squeeze out some money for us all here."

After Frank's passing comment, Dale worried for a moment about Boncanno, then he turned his attention back to Frank's proposal for delivering more product to Tony Di Staccato.

"OK, let me think about this new deal you've got with Staccato. I'll talk to Sammy and let him know what happened to the last shipment and find out what he thinks we should do next. It's going to be hard to satisfy everybody."

Dale gathered up his leftovers, bundled them back into the paper bag and opened the door to get out. He leaned back in to wipe his seat with a napkin, then looked up at Frank.

"You done? I'll throw it out for you."

"Sure, thanks." Frank stuffed his leftovers into the bag and handed it to Dale, then watched him walk to the garbage bins near the exit. Dale came back and got into the Caddy. He adjusted the seat to lean back and clasped his hands together behind his head, staring out the windshield.

"You reminded me, Frank, about Boncanno. He turned out to be a ruthless bastard, who tried to have me killed. Now you tell me he'll likely try again and we're not doing anything to stop him. Susan is still worrying about him and he's dangerous enough to keep me awake at night. But he's small time, compared to this gangster in New York, Tony Di Staccato. How the hell do we not end up worse off with him than we are with Boncanno?"

"Dale, we're off to a good start with Staccato. We're his new best friends. He's so impressed with what we did for him on the first shipment, he handed me twenty thousand for arranging it."

"That just means you owe him now, Frank. He maybe even thinks he owns you and you'll have to do whatever he wants next."

"Nobody owns me, Dale. I only do what I want, for whoever I want. Listen, I know you'd like to get back to business as usual and keep all the criminals out of your life. Unfortunately, they're part of life, yours and everybody else's these days. Your partner Sammy knows that. Our plan has to be how to get along with them, not get hurt, and make some money in the process. Keep it simple, even if it's not easy."

"I know, Frank. You don't have to tell me the ugly facts of life. But I'm trying to keep away from all the gangsters and you keep getting me in deeper, switching from one gang of bad bastards to another."

Frank looked over at him with a big grin. "Am I a great Fixer or what?"

"Not sure who's fixing who here, Frank." Dale said with a grimace. "But let's get back to finding a way to make your deal work and get it over with. Then we can try to move on without getting hurt or getting into more trouble."

"Alright, I'll get back to Staccato and ask him what product he's looking for and you can send his order to Sammy."

"Whoa, whoa. Not so fast. I'll give Sammy a call, but I think I better get over there for a face-to-face meeting on this. There's a lot going on for him. Sammy needs to satisfy the Triads, remember. Switching them to a new customer may not be that easy, if they think we deliberately screwed it up the first time. You can tell Staccato we're working on it and I can pretty much guess what products he'd like. Anything that's currently hot on the market is usually in short supply and hard to get. Buyers don't ask too many questions and they're willing to pay high prices to get what they need. It would be easiest to do small high-value packages, like last time. Not our friggin' monitors in big boxes worth only three hundred dollars apiece."

"Sounds like you've got it all figured out, Dale. You should definitely get into this business."

"No, thanks. That's not the plan. But it's not that complicated. Like any business, you buy as low as possible and sell as high as possible. But like you said, it may be simple, but it's never easy."

"OK," said Frank. "Let's see if we can make this work. I'll call Stack and tell him we're working on it and you can check with Sammy."

Dale took a long breath, exhaled and leaned forward, adjusting his seat to full height again and placed his hand on the dashboard, drumming his fingers quietly. "I'll propose to Sammy that we add product for Stack Distribution in a Chung-Wai monitor shipment to Boston again, but document it properly this time. I don't want to be part of the transaction or sign-off on any of the paperwork, if it's not one-hundred per cent clean. I've already risked getting banned from the U.S. for the last shipment. Maybe worse than that, but I don't want to think about it."

He folded his arms across his chest and continued.

"Sammy can keep whatever he makes on the deal, I don't want any part of it. His Triad contacts in Taiwan, have probably learned by now they need new customers in New York. Let's hope they don't mind shipping to Italians, instead of their Chinese friends. That may be a challenge for Sammy, too."

Frank shrugged. "I'm sure Sammy can be creative enough. Maybe he can offer to buy the goods in Taiwan and the Triads don't have to know where it's going."

"That might work, we'll talk about it."

"OK, I'll drop you back at the office and you can work on your pitch to Sammy. Don't forget to tell him to include me in the transaction. You may not want any part of it, but I like to make money on both sides of the deal."

"I thought you already got paid," said Dale.

"That was for the first job, this is all new business. I have an understanding now with Staccato on his delivery and I'm not greedy. I'll just take a reasonable percentage of whatever you and Sammy can negotiate. I have confidence in you guys."

"Jesus, who's working for who, here?"

Frank looked pleased with himself and wheeled the Caddy out to the street to take Dale back to his office a few blocks away.

14.

Sammy Wong was in his office at Chung-Wai in Taiwan, leaning onto the desk from his high-backed swivel chair. He had the phone to his ear. He pushed aside the long coiled cord that stretched across the green blotter and made a note on the lined writing pad. He shifted to one side and frowned as he listened to Dale, calling from Montreal.

"Yes, Sammy. Your special delivery got picked up in Boston, right after I made the call to the number you gave me. Two guys in a van left with the six cartons. I don't know exactly what happened after that."

Sammy was quizzing Dale after his visit from the angry Triad boss, See Yeung. He had learned from See Yeung that the customers in New Jersey had been robbed and two men had been killed. The Triad operations there were now shut down. See Yeung had been in to see Sammy earlier in the week and was pressing him to find out what went wrong on delivery and whether he and Dale had anything to do with it.

Dale was trying to explain, without saying too much on the phone.

"Look, Sammy, I'm sorry about what happened with See Yeung's shipment and I'd like to propose a way out for you, but it's too complicated to sort out on the phone. I've booked a weekend flight and I can see you in Taipei to discuss it. Let's see what we can arrange. I'm arriving on Flight TA-1754 Tuesday at about 9:30 in the morning. Can you book a hotel and meet me when I arrive?"

Sammy had OK'd the plan.

The flight from Montreal to Taiwan was always a fourteen-hour to sixteen-hour ordeal. Dale had been there many times, but he always found it difficult with the jet lag and adjusting to the time change.

For this trip, he had booked United Air Lines with a connection in Chicago, then an overnight stay in Hong Kong before a short morning flight to Taipei. Chicago was the usual mind-numbing experience navigating through crowds of passengers dragging their luggage through the shabby hallways and departure lounges past the over-priced fast-food counters.

Hong Kong's airport was also busy with crowds of travellers, but it was a smooth and efficient arrival through a modern, architecturally impressive structure with huge windows overlooking the bay and the surrounding harbour.

Dale arrived at about 7:00 PM local time and checked into the Marriot Hotel adjacent to the airport. The hotel was a tall gleaming gold and glass tower with a high-ceilinged lobby decorated with huge Chinese works of art. Dale was ready for a comfortable night's sleep after the cramped confines of the long overnight flight from Chicago. Three in-flight movies had not done much to relieve the boredom. The price of $275-a-night at the Marriott was a bit of a jolt to Dale's travel budget, but arriving at his room and opening the solid mahogany double doors to the sight of a king-sized bed covered with smooth silk sheets and fat pillows piled high, helped to justify his choice for a restful stopover en route to Taiwan.

The next morning his flight departed at eight on China National Airlines and he was up early enough for a call home, before going to breakfast. Susan answered the phone on the second ring.

"Hi, Susie," said Dale, "I wanted to call you guys before flying on to Taipei. Put me on the speaker and I'll say hi to the kids."

"OK, here they are," said Susan.

He heard both their voices. "Hi Daddy!" called Keira, in an excited shriek. Sean mumbled something unintelligible.

"Hey guys," said Dale. He raised his voice for the speaker-phone, "Hello from Hong Kong!"

He heard Sean, a bit louder, but still mumbling. "I thought you were going to Taiwan."

"That's right. I'm flying there soon, but I'm having breakfast here first in Hong Kong. Imagine, you guys are having supper in Montreal on Monday evening and I'm having breakfast in Hong Kong on Tuesday morning. We're thirteen hours ahead of you! Last night, on the plane from Chicago, we crossed an imaginary line called the International Date Line in the middle of the Pacific. It divides today from tomorrow, as the world turns every twenty-four hours. Neat, eh? Check it out with your teacher, Sean. She'll show you on the globe."

"Very interesting geography lesson, Dale," said Susan, "but this phone call must be costing you a fortune."

"Yeah, especially from the hotel room. But I love you guys! You're worth it. I'll call again before I leave Taiwan. *Bonne journée* everybody, have a good day! Bye for now."

The breakfast selection in the Marriott lobby dining room was stunning. Dale browsed the complete buffet area before making his choices from the long rows of steaming stainless steel pots, covered baskets of dim-sum and carefully arranged platters of fresh seafood. He filled one large and one small plate with a variety of steamed dumplings, shrimp, spicy meatballs, rice noodles and chow mein.

When in Rome, do as the Romans, and when in China, well ... I'm getting better at using chopsticks.

He realized, as he looked out the window by his table over the bustling Hong Kong harbour, that he was not actually in China. Hong Kong would remain British territory until the ninety-nine-year lease of the territory would end in 1997.

That should be an interesting transition. From an independent British colony to a city-state in Red China controlled by a Communist dictatorship. The Communists, he remembered, had fought under Mao Zedong against Chiang Kai-shek and the Nationalist Chinese and drove them out of mainland China to the island of Formosa, where they established the Democratic Republic of China, better known now, as Taiwan. It was still claimed, by the Communist Peoples Republic of modern China, to be part of their country.

Dale thought he should ask Sammy's opinion on the current politics of the region, regarding China, Hong Kong and Taiwan. It might be a welcome change of subject from their discussions on how to get away with smuggling stolen computer products into the United States.

*****

Later that day in Taiwan, Dale was sitting in Sammy's office above the front entrance to the Chung-Wai Manufacturing facilities off Hang-Sen Road on the outskirts of Taipei.

They were relaxed in plush armchairs with bright flowered patterns of red, yellow and blue on white cotton wrapped around dark red polished wood. Two additional empty chairs were set back from the large carved ebony coffee table. The table had a tray on it with an assortment of sweet snacks and a large ceramic tea pot with two small cups of tea. Wisps of steam rose from the tea cups.

Now that they were in private and face-to-face, Dale had explained the whole story of the shipment to Boston and what Frank had arranged with Tony Di Staccato in New York. Sammy's frown deepened as the story progressed to the events in New Jersey, culminating in the raid and killing of Triad members by Staccato's gang.

"Our intent, Sammy, was simply to make it a losing proposition for the Triads. They were pushing us to do something we didn't want to do and I thought we were at risk of getting caught for it. I wanted to push the whole thing away from us, if possible. We were taking a helluva risk helping them smuggle product into the States."

"But you took the risk of getting us killed for screwing it up," said Sammy. "I'm not sure they're convinced we didn't have something to do with it."

"Yes, that was the chance I took. But now we can put it right for everybody involved and get it under control. You can even make a few bucks on the side this time, Sammy."

"You always find a way to make a buck, Dale, but this is very dangerous business we're getting into here."

"I know I took some risks for us," said Dale, "but I'm trying to find a way to get you out of this business. That's why I'm here now to help you shift the Triads to these guys in New York. Frank has set it up with Tony Di Staccato and he thinks we can get you off the hook with the Triads. Staccato's the Mafia gang leader in New York who grabbed the first shipment and now he wants more. Frank is trying to persuade us to make the deal."

"Who is this guy, Frank? Where did he come from?"

"Ah, Frank the Fixer, he's called. He has quite a story. His real name is Faysal Mohamed Abou. He came to Montreal at about seventeen as a refugee from Somalia. Frank was smart enough to escape from there and settle himself in Montreal. He does pretty well on his own and manages to work both sides of the law to his advantage. Sometimes he helps the cops with tactics they can't use themselves and sometimes he does dirty work for the criminals. You may remember him as the guy who got me away from Gino Boncanno and moved me to the Renaldi family for protection and financing, until you stepped up, Sammy, for the half million I needed.

Boncanno didn't take it very well, and he tried to have me killed in a fake robbery attempt. Fortunately, Frank saw it coming and saved my life."

Sammy nodded thoughtfully. "Sounds like another good friend and partner for you, Dale. I'd like to meet him next time I'm in Montreal."

"Absolutely Sammy, he'll be your partner now, too. In fact, I'm trying to leave the two of you alone to work this out, so I can get back to the computer business in Montreal and Boston. I'd prefer to take care of that for us, instead. So let's work out how to deliver more product to Staccato in New York. If we can get the product he wants at the price he wants, I'll get the message to Frank and he'll arrange with Staccato for him to pay before you deliver. I don't even have to be part of it. You can ship a container directly to him in New Jersey and you're done. Once and for all, we hope. If you fill the container with monitors, I'm sure he can sell those, too. Does that work for you?"

Sammy stirred his tea and then took a long, slow sip. "It works OK for me, but what's more important, does it work for See Yeung? I'll call him tomorrow and we'll find out what he's willing to do."

"All right, that sounds like a plan. Can we go for dinner now? I'm buying, but you can pick the spot."

They went to a favourite restaurant of Sammy's near Dale's hotel. Dinner was a few simple dishes of spicy food, washed down with Tsingtao beer. After dinner, they skipped their usual visit to the disco. Dale decided he needed another quiet night, rather than visiting Sammy's club with the loud disco music and drinking that inevitably went long into the night. He didn't need to make the next day more difficult. They planned to discuss how to tell their story and make a proposal to See Yeung and the Triads to eventually end the smuggling, if possible.

As they arrived at Chung-Wai in Sammy's chauffeur driven Mercedes the next morning, he suggested they visit the factory before going back to his office.

"Let me show you what's new in production, Dale, I think you'll be impressed. You still want monitors again after we get out of the smuggling business, right?"

"Hell, yes," said Dale, "the sooner the better."

They walked through the visitor reception area and entered the factory through a secure door protected by a key code. Sammy punched in the numbers and opened the door that let them directly into the manufacturing plant. A high ceiling with hanging fluorescent lights extended over the wide array of rolling conveyors and work stations with some open offices along the near wall. The first section of production was dedicated to circuit board assembly with ladies in white uniforms and hair nets sitting on stools on either side of a slow moving conveyor, installing components on the boards that passed in front of them. The circuit boards then rumbled up into the wave solder machine to fix the components into place. Toxic fumes from the soldering process were sucked up into a wide fume hood with aluminum wrapped ducts leading to vents on the roof.

Along the back cement-block wall was the final packing and shipping area. Monitor boxes were stacked on pallets and a gas powered forklift ran back and forth from the loading dock, manoeuvering the pallets into a forty-foot container. Inside the container, two workers were lifting the boxes off the pallets and stacking them tightly to get the maximum quantity into the shipment. The boxes were all marked CHW for Chung-Wai's branded product.

Dale did not see any EXL monitors in production and asked Sammy when the next shipment would be scheduled.

"Starting next week, we're doing a run of three containers to Canada for you. But come on over to the QA department, Dale, I have something to show you in testing. It's our first 17-inch monitor."

Sammy picked up his pace as he led Dale into a closed off area beside the final assembly section. He stopped inside and pointed at a large monitor with a flat black glass screen sitting on the bench in front of a technician with the plastic back cover off for access to the components on the open chassis. The technician was running test patterns and Dale peered at the fine lines and bright colours on the screen.

"It's gorgeous, Sammy, when will you be shipping it? Looks like a money-maker to me. Have you got costing for us yet?"

Sammy nodded and smiled at the technician. "Glad you like it, Dale, but we need to finish testing and tuning it first. We want to be sure you're going to be happy with it before we ship anyone the samples. We have parts on order to go into production in three months. You'll be among the first to get them. Don't worry about the cost, we'll be a lot lower than anybody else and it's the same high quality screens from Hitachi and Toshiba that they're using in their own monitors from Japan. Your old supplier, Korea Computer Systems has nothing like this for you either, I'm sure."

"Attaboy, Sammy, staying ahead on price and delivery. Keep it up, we appreciate it. Keeps us all happy and making money."

Sammy grinned, as they headed back out of the factory and returned to Sammy's office on the second floor where fresh coffee was waiting for them.

"Black for me, thanks," said Dale, as Sammy looked up before filling his cup. Dale blew on it and sipped carefully before sitting back in his armchair and returning to their discussion.

"OK, Sammy, now that we've looked after the regular business of monitors in Montreal and Boston, let's talk about our new customer in New York. Frank made promises we have to keep. These guys don't like to be disappointed any more than your Triads do. I'm not sure who is more dangerous and I don't want to find out."

He leaned forward, elbows on his knees, hands clasped.

"Frank thinks we should make the most of the opportunity and milk it for all it's worth. He thinks I'm a shitty business partner for not getting involved, but I just want to get back to the legitimate business of selling computer products through regular channels at a reasonable price. I don't want to be dealing in stolen product, any more. I know my way seems slow and boring to some people, but at least I don't risk going to jail or getting killed and I can be proud to tell my kids what I actually do for a living. This detour into smuggling is a distraction I want to avoid, so let's find a way to satisfy them quickly and end it."

"The Triads are not going to let go of me very easily," said Sammy, "I've been working with See Yeung for a long time. I agree about trying to stay out of jail and not getting killed, though. Boring and slow sounds good to me, too."

They both sipped their coffee and contemplated their options. Dale put his cup down and glanced around the low table in front of him to busy his restless hands with something. He picked up the coffee spoon and slowly stirred his black coffee.

"OK Sammy, let me explain what we're dealing with in New York, then you can tell me about your guys at this end. Frank arranged with Tony Di Staccato to look after the first shipment to Boston from the Triads. Staccato does lots of business in stolen computer products all up and down the East Coast of the U.S. His guys followed the shipment after it was delivered from our warehouse in Boston to the Triads warehouse in New Jersey, then they came back there the next night. Pretty violent exchange, like I said, but it was a good haul and Staccato probably picked up close to a million dollars in computer parts. He was very happy about it and dropped twenty grand into Frank's pocket for the pleasure of doing business with us. He wants to do more of the same and Frank thinks we should do it."

"You think this Tony Staccato will be satisfied with just one more shipment?"

"No, probably not. But maybe we can explain the supply has dried up. I dunno. He liked the mix of CPUs and micro drives, if we can do that again. Maybe some other high value product, like video cards. They would be easy to explain in a container shipment full of monitors."

Sammy considered what he was hearing from Dale. "I think our problem is that See Yeung doesn't trust us anymore. He thinks we deliberately screwed it up and cost him his product and his customer."

"Maybe I need to talk to him and give him a better version of the story," said Dale.

"You really want to meet these guys?"

"Not really and I don't intend to give them my name and home address. Let's just introduce me as your guy from Boston, to explain what happened. I'll tell him we want to fix the problem and make another delivery for him to New York. We can take it from there and see what happens."

"OK," said Sammy, "It'll be an interesting meeting. I'll set it up for this evening and try to get a guarantee we walk out of there alive when it's over."

"Good point," said Dale, clenching his jaw. "I'm feeling better about this idea already." He shook his head with a shudder. "Jesus, Sammy, you trying to scare the shit out of me now?"

Sammy laughed. "No, no. I'm just continuing your training in Taiwan business practices. If it's not a good deal, somebody gets killed. I'm sure you'll learn something useful you can take back home."

"Whatever I take back home, I hope it's not that. Go ahead and set it up, then. You can pick me up at the hotel later. I'll take a taxi back now and get some work done until I hear from you."

"OK, I'll call you there, when it's set up."

*****

Back in his hotel room, Dale was not doing any work. He was lying on the bed staring at the ceiling and wondering what he had gotten himself into.

What the hell am I thinking? I'm ten thousand miles from home in a foreign country. I don't speak the language and know nothing about the culture. I invite myself to meet the leader of these murderous Triads? Goddamn it, how did Frank talk me into this? I should be running for cover and staying away from Taiwan and the Triads altogether!

Early in the evening, Dale was picked up at the hotel by Sammy and his driver in the Mercedes for the meeting with See Yeung. They drove only a few blocks through the heavy traffic of noisy cars along with the motorbikes and scooters belching black smoke into the air. The driver pulled up at the entrance to a narrow street full of pedestrians wandering between open food-stalls on both sides of the street. The vendors were all gesticulating over the steaming trays of freshly cooked seafood, beef, pork and chicken from the smoking grills and steaming pots behind them.

"We can walk from here," said Sammy. "He'll park at the other end of the street and pick us up there, later."

They started between the stalls shuffling along with the crowd. Dale was fascinated by the stall with a row of freshly gutted snakes hanging from a pole across the back, dripping blood into small bowls on the shelf below. He stopped before bumping into Sammy, who was pointing to a small bowl full of the red liquid. He looked at Dale.

"Really good for your sex life, want some?"

"No thanks," said Dale, "I don't need any help."

"Me neither," said Sammy with a grin. He turned to the vendor and ordered two skewers of grilled snake. He pointed to the grill and turned to Dale with raised eyebrows to inquire if he wanted some of that.

Dale shook his head, "I prefer shrimp on a stick to snake on a stake."

Sammy smiled. "OK, you'll find shrimp further on."

After Dale had made his choice among the tempting delicacies, trying to ensure that he knew what he was eating, they continued down the street, munching on their skewers. Dale spit into his paper napkin the unshelled shrimp that he almost gagged on trying to swallow.

At the end of the first section of street vendors, they sat on a bench with their bottles of beer and looked at the passersby and the restaurants that continued to the end of the block.

"See Yeung is upstairs there, at the Jade Queen," said Sammy, with a nod further down the street.

Dale saw the name on a bright yellow and green neon sign a few doors down. There were two heavy set men in black suits lounging at the front door.

"You ready?"

"Let's do it," said Dale.

They drained their beers, tossed the bottles in a nearby trash can and walked to the door of the Jade Queen.

Sammy had a few words with one of the heavies and they walked in through the restaurant and upstairs to the end of the hall. Two more strong-men in suits stood on either side of the door. This time they were frisked, before the door was opened for them.

They stepped into a brightly lit, colourfully decorated private room. There was a large round table in the centre covered with dirty dishes and leftovers in front of a large round man, whose hands were wrapped around a long rack of spare ribs that he was pulling apart. He dropped the ribs onto the overflowing plate in front of him and wiped his hands on the white napkin that he pulled from under the folds of his neck.

See Yeung rolled his chair back from the table and indicated the two empty chairs to his left for Sammy and Dale. He was alone in the room.

He spoke to Sammy in Mandarin. There was a brief exchange before Sammy turned to Dale and switched to English. "This is Mr. See Yeung. I explained that you are my friend from Boston, who received the shipment from us last month. You can explain what happened in English."

See Yeung then spoke for himself, in clear English. "So Mr. Boston, what happened to my shipment?"

Dale cleared his throat, still irritated by the shrimp shell that had stuck there. "Mr. Yeung, I want to assure you, we received the shipment as planned and delivered it, exactly as you requested. Two gentlemen came to our warehouse and picked up the six boxes in their minivan. I don't know what happened after that, but Sammy tells me that apparently in New Jersey, some gangsters broke into your customer's warehouse and stole the product from them in a big shoot-out."

See Yeung frowned. "And you had nothing to do with that?"

"Hell no, I wanted nothing to do with any of this. I just wanted to do what Sammy asked me to do to satisfy you and not make any trouble for anybody."

"Well, I am not satisfied and I do not believe you," said See Yeung. "I have lost the product and my payment. People were killed and now I have no customers in New Jersey."

"Well, you'll have to believe me, because it's the truth. I had nothing to do with the break-in or the shoot-out. I'm sorry it didn't go according to plan. Maybe we can make it up to you with a new customer."

See Yeung kept his eyes on him, as Dale continued. "The people who took the product from you, somehow they figured out we delivered the stolen goods from Taiwan. They've approached us for more product and threatened us now too, if we don't deliver. They'll pay a good price, if you can get more of the same."

See Yeung frowned at them both.

"We do not have *stolen goods*, as you say. We have products delivered to us in exchange for our services, like we do for your friend here, Mr. Wong. We have lots of product, but we will not sell to the people you are now working with. They're Mafia from New York, right?"

"Yes, I think so. But apparently they have a business in computer products and can move a lot of stock."

"No. We do not do business with those people. Especially after they have killed some of my friends. Would you do that?"

"No, I understand. So what do you suggest we can do to satisfy you?"

"I do not wish to do more business with you. I will make new arrangements with Mr. Wong. It is not your problem."

Dale looked to Sammy to respond.

"Thank you, See Yeung," he said. "Thank you for meeting with us and giving my friend a chance to explain. We wanted to try to make it right after the problems with your delivery. We can talk about our other arrangements, whenever you wish. Perhaps we can do a shipment to California with our containers that are going there."

"We will talk about it another day," said See Yeung, "Goodbye, to you both."

He pulled himself back to the table, reached for the rack of spare ribs and scanned the dishes for any more appealing leftovers.

Dale and Sammy got up and walked back out through the restaurant and into the street.

"OK, now I need a real dinner," said Dale, exhaling a long breath. "Then we can work on a new plan for Frank."

They went back to Sammy's favourite restaurant after the driver met them at the end of the street. They sat quietly at a small table in back, far from the other diners. They had more Tsingtao beer and waited for the food that Sammy had ordered for them.

"Sorry I couldn't persuade him to work with us, Sammy. Do you think you can satisfy him with a new arrangement to keep him off your back?"

"Yeah, I think I'll be OK. I'll offer to slip some of his special deliveries into the California shipments. He has customers there too, I'm sure.

"OK. I hope it works out for you, but I still have a problem to satisfy Staccato. He's still looking for product in New York, remember?"

"I have an idea for you there," said Sammy, pushing a plate of steaming noodles and vegetables towards Dale. "You mentioned video cards. I think I can get you some of the latest ATI cards, worth about $1200 dollars each, at a very special price for Staccato."

"How is that possible? ATI cards are always in short supply with everybody screaming for them. We do a lot of business with ATI and I have a very good relationship with the President and owner, K.Y. Ho. I wouldn't want to be part of any stealing from him. That's a step too far for me."

"But Dale, as See Yeung explained, it's not really stealing, it's just another arrangement made by the manufacturers here in Taiwan. Most of their customers, like ATI, know what's going on. They don't approve it, they just ignore it. It helps them get better costs from the manufacturer and everybody is happy to sprinkle a few gems into the black market."

Dale looked unconvinced, so Sammy continued.

"Let me explain. The manufacturer for ATI here is Taipei Micro Devices, TMD. I know the owner well. Terry Chou is an old friend from school days. We actually started our first business together, selling brand name knock-offs from Hong Kong, like Rolex watches and RayBan sunglasses. Made some good money for a while. Then we got greedy and into selling drugs, mostly opium from China. We were making even more money, until the Triads showed up and scared us right out of business. Terry and I went back to school and on to university, investing our money more wisely. But we met See Yeung back in those days and he seems to still like doing business with us."

"Interesting," said Dale, "Not the first young entrepreneurs I've known who got started on the shady side of business. But what do you think Terry Chou can do for us now?"

"Well, like I said, he builds a lot of ATI product and it doesn't all go to ATI. Some he pushes off the line and gives to the Triads for their purposes. I'll tell him about the trouble we have making your deal with New York and I'm sure he can get us some ATI product."

"That would work for Frank and Tony Di Staccato," said Dale, "but I'm really not happy to be dealing in stolen or counterfeit ATI product. K.Y. Ho has been very good to me and I've made a lot of money with ATI." He had nothing to add and sat glumly staring into his plate.

"I appreciate your loyalty to a supplier, Dale, but I'm sure your friend at ATI is wise enough to know what's going on and would forgive you if he knew the jam you're in. He worked in Taiwan a few years himself, right? That's how he knows Terry Chou and how business is done here. You're just getting your introduction now."

Dale looked up at Sammy and nodded, looking very uncomfortable. *This is going to have to be the solution, I guess.*

"OK, we'll try it, but one shipment only, then we're done with our New York customers and your Triad friends."

Dale dropped the chopsticks he had been using and plunged a big fork into his plate of rice noodles and shrimp.

15.

After his return from Taiwan and a long, tiring day back at the office in Montreal, Dale came home in the early evening and pulled into the driveway. He lifted his heavy briefcase off the passenger seat and got out, heading toward the front steps.

"Hi, Mr. Hunter," he heard from behind him.

He turned to see young Lawrence Baldwin, son of the neighbours next door, standing on the lawn between their driveways.

"Hi, Lawrence, how are you?"

"I'm fine, thank you. But I wonder if I could talk to you, Mr. Hunter. I have some questions I'd like to ask you about running my own business."

"Really, you're thinking about running your own business? How old are you, Lawrence?"

"I'm fourteen. I'm starting a lawn mowing business this summer, when school's out. I want to have my own business someday, like you."

"That's pretty ambitious, Lawrence. Why don't you just enjoy the summer holidays, instead. Forget about running your own business. Work hard at school, then go on to university and become an engineer or a lawyer or a doctor. That's easier than running your own business."

"Well, my parents did that. My dad's an engineer and my mom's a teacher. They both have good jobs, but they're tired of working for somebody else. They have to do what they're told all the time and can't do what they really want."

Dale was surprised by Lawrence's comments about his parents. *They seem pretty happy to me. Always home for dinner, never working weekends. They've really given their son the wrong impression of life running your own business. Nobody ever tells you what to do, eh?*

"My dad said I should talk to you. Mom agrees. You seem to be doing pretty well in your own business, nice car and everything."

"So you want a nice car and you think you should run your own business to get one?"

"No, I just want to be my own boss. So I can do what I want."

"I see. Well, that's a better answer. Tell me some more about what you have in mind."

Dale sat down on the front steps and waited for Lawrence to reply.

"OK, here's my plan. The business is called Larry's Landscaping for Lovely Lawns and I'll take care of peoples' yards for the summer."

"Good name, Lawrence, but it'll be hard to fit on a business card, especially if you do it in French and English. We're calling you Larry, now?"

"Yeah, it's catchy, eh?" Lawrence was getting animated. "I'll be ready with bilingual business cards and flyers, pretty soon. I'm thinking I'll drop a flyer in everybody's mailbox next week, then start knocking on doors and follow-up."

"OK, you're organised. Sounds like a good start. I'd suggest a door hanger instead of flyers in the mailbox. It's harder to ignore and doesn't get lost in all the junk mail. Tell you what, Larry of Larry's Lovely Landscaping," said Dale with a smile. "I'll help you with your plans, but you're not trying to sell me shares in the business are you?"

Now Lawrence was grinning back at him. "No, not yet. I don't need any money. My Dad's letting me use our lawnmower and he's paying for the business cards and flyers. But I'd really appreciate your help, Mr. Hunter."

"OK, you're planning to sell lawn care to the neighbours. Let's have a look at your numbers for all the costs and your expected sales to see if you can make any money in this business of yours. Can you come back and see me on the weekend with some numbers?"

"Yes, sir. I'll work on it and see you on the weekend. Thanks, Mr. Hunter."

Lawrence reached out with a vigorous and surprisingly firm handshake for a fourteen-year-old.

16

Two weeks later, after Dale had explained to Frank what Sammy had proposed in Taiwan, Frank the Fixer was back in the offices of Stack Distribution in New Jersey. He and Tony Di Staccato sat in the same pair of wooden chairs facing the desk of Pat Cametti.

Frank instinctively scanned and catalogued the potential threats around him. Against the wall off to one side were the same twin tough guys in suits, each resting an arm on the small table between them. Frank recognized one as Carlo, whom he had met in Boston before following the minivan to New Jersey, then again at Tony's when he'd gone there for dinner. The man beside him was bigger than Frank and looked mean and tough, ready to exercise physical force at the slightest provocation. Frank kept the two bodyguards in his peripheral vision.

Everyone listened closely as he explained his proposition to them. "My friend in Boston just came back from Taiwan and he's made a deal with his partner over there to look after your request for more product. The first thing you should know, though, is that we are only going to be able to make one shipment. It's hard to get computer products anywhere these days, legal or otherwise, because the newest stuff is all in such tight supply. The Triads in Taipei are not co-operating, either. The guy who made the original shipment refuses to do business with us at any price, especially if we're shipping the product to you. Apparently they're kind of stubborn about that and loyal to their Chinese buddies. And not too happy about them getting shot up and shut down by you guys, two months ago."

"No shit," said Pat, "Why'd you have to tell 'em we were the customers?"

"We didn't have to tell them," said Frank. "They figured it out and they're convinced we set it up, so they don't trust us, either. They're still beating on our partner in Taiwan to make it up to them."

Pat looked at Tony. "Maybe we should go over there and put another beating on them, so they leave our friends alone."

"Forget about 'em," said Tony. "Leave 'em alone over there in their own dirty little pig pen. We've got enough to do here, keeping them out of our backyard in the States." He turned to look at Frank. "So how you gonna look after us then?"

"We've made another arrangement to get you some high value product that'll be easy to sell. You should do very well with it. You know a company, called ATI? They make video cards."

Tony looked at Pat, who nodded once and said, "Of course."

"Well they've just launched a new product called the Rage, that's all the rage," said Frank. "Sounds dumb, I know, but apparently they're even better at marketing than they are at making high-priced video cards. Anyway, our guy over there is close to the owner of the company that builds for ATI in Taiwan. The Triads won't co-operate with us, but this guy will. Apparently, he's already pretty good at building a few extra pieces that fall off the truck into other people's hands, like ours, if we want it. He can get us one good shipment, but that's it. There's a limit to how much they can spill over the sides without losing their ATI business. We figure we can get you about a half million dollars' worth, at current wholesale prices."

Frank paused and looked at Pat, then Tony before continuing. "We'll confirm exactly what we have when we have it and then we'll give you a price for the lot. If you agree and send the cash by wire transfer in advance, we'll put it in a container with a shipment of monitors. All the paperwork will be clean and legitimate, so we'll have no problems at customs clearance or inspection coming into the U.S."

"How can you do that, if it's stolen or counterfeit product?" asked Pat.

"It's not counterfeit," said Frank, "it's the real thing. ATI original manufactured product with full retail packaging and we'll show the real price on the customs documents. The guys in manufacturing over there run a bunch of duplicate serial numbers and nobody can tell the difference. Might be a problem if somebody calls in a warranty claim and the serial number has already come up. By then, it'll be too late and too hard to trace it back anywhere. I think we've got you covered. But you'll have to settle for the one shipment and on those terms."

Tony looked angry. "You got a lotta nerve, kid, coming in here and dictating terms to us, alone and unarmed. What're you gonna do, if Pauli here pulls a gun on you and we start dictating the terms."

Pauli was the bigger thug at the table against the wall. He hoisted himself up out of the chair and stood to glare at Frank, revealing the holster and protruding gun butt under his jacket. He leaned back on his heels and crossed his arms above his fat belly.

Frank looked over his shoulder at him, then turned to Tony. "I'd just have to take it away from him, before he hurts somebody."

Pauli's face flushed in anger. He stepped toward Frank and reached for his gun. "What'd you say, kid?"

Frank leapt up from his chair, spun around on the balls of his feet and smashed his left forearm into Pauli's throat.

The big man choked out a cough and started to fall backwards. Frank drove a hard right fist into his extended belly and Pauli snapped upright again, coughing harder. Frank grabbed the shoulders of his suit jacket and pulled him face down toward his rising knee. Frank smashed his knee into Pauli's face and then threw him backwards up against the wall. The back of his head thumped on the wall and he slid down it, dazed, onto the floor.

His hand came up to clutch his broken bleeding nose and he rolled over onto one elbow. He looked up to see Frank standing over him, holding his gun and casually pointing it at him.

Carlo was standing with his gun held out at arm's length, aimed with both hands at Frank's chest, but standing well away from him. Pat Cametti was standing with both hands gripping the front of his desk, fingers on top, no gun in sight. Cametti looked from Frank to Pauli on the floor and then to Tony Di Staccato, who still sat with his leg crossed over his knee.

Tony looked at Cametti and spoke quietly from his chair. "I think he made his point."

He shook his head and held out his hand for the revolver in Frank's hand.

Frank placed it carefully on the far corner of the desk away from Pauli. *He just might be stupid or humiliated enough to reach for it again.* Frank went back to his chair and sat down again beside Tony.

Pat Cametti dropped into the chair behind his desk and Carlo put his gun back in the holster and sat down, too. Pauli pulled himself up into his chair beside the table and held a handkerchief to his bloody nose, staring at Frank above the white folds.

Frank had a momentary Ku Klux Klan image flash in his mind. *OK, guess I got a round in for my African American cousins.*

Staccato turned to Frank and said, "OK, we have the story straight, only one more shipment from Taiwan. Let us know when it's ready. But you still owe me, Frank, after dropping twenty grand on you, last visit. So, I'm wondering, what else can you do for me? You still driving the big Caddy?"

"Yeah, it goes where I go," said Frank.

"Fine," said Tony. "I know some pretty good hiding places in a Caddy and we have a shipment I can prepare for you to take back to Canada."

"Sorry, Tony, I don't do that kinda work. I don't really want the drug dogs sniffing around my car and the border agents ripping it apart."

"Yuh know, Frank, you're really getting to be a pain in the ass," Tony snarled. "I thought we were going to do business together. Now, I think you should just fuck-off back to Canada and don't come here again, unless you're invited."

"Well, I can leave, all right," said Frank, "but I can't promise not to come back. I don't always go where I'm invited and I don't always get invited where I decide to go. Kind of an independent asshole, I guess."

Tony was shaking his head. "You get away with a lot, Frank." He was having trouble restraining a smile. "Look, I like you and I think we can use you. I'm gonna put you in touch with my cousin in Montreal and you can work it out with him. Maybe he'll have something useful you can dirty your hands with. Gimme a call next week. Now, get outta here."

Frank stood, straightened his leather jacket, nodded at Pat Cametti, turned his back to the scowls of Pauli and Carlo and walked out the door, closing it quietly behind him.

Tony turned to look with disgust at Pauli, still hunched over awkwardly in his chair.

"You useless piece of shit. That's the best you can do for me?"

17.

"OK, Lawrence, let's have a look at your numbers."

They were sitting at the picnic table on Dale's patio at the back of the house. Young Lawrence had pushed his spiral notebook towards Dale, open to a page neatly covered with notes and calculations.

"Who's going to work for five-dollars-an-hour?" said Dale. "Sean might, but he's too young to push a power mower around anybody's yard."

"No, I'm not," came a voice from the house.

They looked up to see Sean standing in the kitchen, looking out at them through the screen door.

"OK, Sean, come on out. Maybe Lawrence has a job for you. You might accidently learn something about business, too. We're talking about his plans for Larry's Lovely Landscaping. Sounds good already, eh?"

Sean quickly slid the screen door open and closed it behind him. He came down the steps to the patio and sat down on the picnic table bench beside Lawrence, opposite Dale. He placed his elbows on the table with his chin in his hands, keeping his eyes on his Dad.

Lawrence pointed to the page that Dale was looking at. "It's OK, Mr. Hunter, I know I have to make a profit. That's what I calculated here. Let me show you."

"Making a profit's good, Lawrence, not evil like a lot of people think, but there's more to running a business than making a profit."

Dale switched to a gruff old man's voice as he continued. "Don't you know Rule Number One, kid?" He put on a stern face and looked first at Lawrence, then at Sean, then back at Lawrence. "Rule Number One is, 'Don't trust nobody!'"

"Oh," said Lawrence. He and Sean both looked confused.

Dale switched back to his own voice. "Don't worry, boys. It's actually not true. Just the opposite. In business, you have to trust everybody or you'll never get anywhere. You have to trust your employees to show up every day and work hard without lying, cheating or stealing from you. You have to trust your customers to pay for what you deliver. You have trust your suppliers to deliver what they promised. And you have to trust the government not to change the rules on you. And then, they all have to trust you to do what you say you're going to do."

"Oh. OK, now I get it. Sounds complicated," said Lawrence. "How do I know who I can trust?"

"That's where you have to be careful and make good choices. Four steps, that's the way I do it."

Dale held his hand up with four fingers facing the boys. "First, you have to know who you're dealing with. Second, you have to decide if you like them and want to do business with them. Third, decide if you can respect them, for who they are and what they can do for you. Fourth, can you trust them? So, remember the four steps. Know, like, respect and trust, always in that order. And remember also, everybody you want to do business with is going through the same process for you. Who are you? Do they like you? Do they respect what you know and what you can deliver? Do they trust you to deliver what you promise?

The boys looked at each other. Lawrence nodded and Sean looked proud of his Dad.

"So remember those four steps," said Dale, "and you won't go too far wrong. It may take some time before you know for sure if you can trust somebody, and if you can't you have to end it quickly."

Dale's mind wandered back over the memories of some of his own bad experiences. *Nobody warned me to watch out for lying, cheating employees, customers and suppliers. It's hard to know who to trust and always painful and expensive when they let you down.*

"Mr. Hunter?" Lawrence interrupted Dale's train of thought. He and Sean were both looking at him.

"Yeah, sorry. OK, let's look at your numbers again." He reached for the notebook. "Five dollars an hour is still a problem. You might as well work for someone else's lawn care company at minimum wage or just sling hamburgers at McDonald's. Running your own business will be more fun than that, but it should also be more profitable."

He turned the page and held his hand out for Lawrence's pencil to start making his own calculations. "Let's try paying yourself at least seven dollars an hour and see if we can cover all your other costs, too. I know your dad is loaning you the lawnmower for no charge, but what about gas for the mower, fertilizer and pesticides? And paying Sean to help you out? Are you buying steel-toed safety boots, by the way? I don't want to see either of you lose any toes on the job."

Lawrence looked concerned again as Dale continued. "Have you thought about what's most important to you and to the customer? Are some of them willing to pay more for special treatment? Do they care about health and safety for their property or their kids? Or the environment? Maybe they'll pay extra for safe, environmentally friendly lawn care, without any harmful chemicals or pesticides."

Dale wrote some more notes on the page and handed the notebook back to Lawrence. "I think you'll be able to look after a few neighbours and make a few bucks, Lawrence. Let's not make it too complicated. Here's my suggestion for what to charge for a single mowing of a typical lawn and what to charge for the whole summer."

Lawrence peered at the page and nodded his approval. "OK, I'll finish my advertising flyers and start knocking on doors."

"Good. I'm happy to sign up as your first customer. You can start training Sean here too, so he can make all the mistakes at home. It's close to the first aid kit, in case he whacks off a toe."

Dale reached over the table to shake Lawrence's hand. Lawrence gathered up his notebook and went back next door.

Dale turned to his son. "What do you think?"

Sean shrugged. "I'm sure I can help him make some money. And don't worry, Dad, I'll take care of my toes." He got up to go back inside.

Dale followed, wondering if his son would be an entrepreneur too, one day. *Maybe he has a future in the landscaping business.*

18.

"Nice to meet in my office for a change," said Dale, "instead of hanging out in our cars or cheap restaurants. Don't you agree?"

They'd just completed a quick tour of the facilities of 3D Computer Products through the warehouse and service department and were now sitting in Dale's office.

"Well, you know," said Frank, "I never really enjoy squeezing into that tiny sports coupe of yours and the cheap restaurants are always your choice, not mine."

"What can I say? I've got to watch the cash flow. It's not easy come, easy go, like you think. But now you know, Frank, what I really do for a living. I hope you learned something useful. Maybe we can get you a job in a real business like this and away from the criminal crap you're always mixed up in."

"But Dale, it's hard to make a buck in any real business. I'm doing too well on my own to get a real job, especially with some hard-ass businessman like you squeezing me to work too hard and paying me too little."

"I'm not that kind of businessman, Frank. Ask anybody here. Best boss they ever had."

"And how much do you have to pay them to say that?"

Good question. It's hard to know if they're really happy here or just sucking up to get treated a little better.

"Don't worry, Frank, I'm not making you an offer."

"And I'm not asking," said Frank. "However ..." he let the phrase hang in the air before continuing. "I do have an interesting offer for you."

Dale was already shaking his head. "Oh boy, here comes another one of your bad ideas to get me to play along with the crooks and gangsters in your life. Before you go any further, let me remind you, Frank, I'm just a regular guy trying to make an honest living in my own business. I don't want to have to lie, cheat or steal to get ahead. I love to win at the game, but I'm a bit stubborn, maybe a bit stupid, about playing by the rules. I know my customers and my suppliers want me to push the limits, like they do, but I prefer to win playing by the rules."

Now Frank was shaking his head and looking skeptical. "Yeah, yeah, I know Dale. I've heard your speech before. A few times. But you know the real world is not that simple. It's too late for you to convert me to your religion and I'm not trying to convert you to mine, either. I just want you to be practical and consider the opportunity I'm giving you."

Dale was shaking his head again. The raised eyebrows suggested to Frank that he was ready to listen.

"OK, now listen up," he said. "There's a couple of possibilities for us to look at. We're still partners in business and crime, right?"

"Business, yes. Crime, I'm trying to quit," replied Dale.

"I know, but quitting is not as easy as you'd like, once we're into it. I made the pitch to Tony Di Staccato, like we agreed. Only one shipment and on our terms. He was ready to kill me for it. He may still want to kill me after it's done. So I'd like to try a little harder to keep him happy."

"Fine, but these are your friends, Frank, not mine. You'll have to manage them on your own."

"Well, that's what I'm doing. And Tony's having second thoughts, anyway. He's decided he's already got better suppliers than us on the East Coast. However…" he paused again, for effect. Dale was rolling his eyes at him.

"However, he wants us to help him do more business on the West Coast in California, where there's lots of action and he thinks he's missing out."

Dale responded. "Why don't we just get out of his way and let him find somebody else who can deliver for him? You should find something else too, Frank, before this gets any more complicated and dangerous."

"That's what I'm trying to do," said Frank. "Tony has introduced me to his cousin here, Giuseppe Luciano, another very successful Montreal businessman and another good connection for me. You may have read about him in the papers, they call him 'Lucky Joey' Luciano."

Dale dropped his head in his hands, elbows on his desk. "Man, oh man. You really are determined to get in deeper with the Mafia. Of course, I've read about him. He gets a lot of press in the crime pages of *Le Journal de Montréal*. I'm hating your idea more all the time.

"But you haven't heard it yet," said Frank. He reached for his empty coffee cup. "Let's refill, then we can get serious for a bit."

He got up and started for the kitchen down the hall and the coffee pot that he'd seen earlier. Dale grabbed his own EXL mug off the desk. It was still half full, but cold now. He followed Frank to the kitchen. The office was quiet with only two other people at their desks. It was well after five.

They went back to Dale's office and he closed the door behind them.

Frank resumed. "OK, Dale, now pay attention. I met with Luciano last week. He's excited by what he learned from Tony and Stack Distribution. He's ready to get into the computer business, himself. Apparently people are making a lot of money in this business, Dale. I don't know what's wrong with you."

Dale declined to bite and Frank continued. "So, Luciano would like us to deliver a few shipments to him here in Montreal. You think you could arrange that?"

"Absolutely not! Not now, not ever." Dale pushed himself back from the table and threw up his hands.

"Dammit, Frank, what the hell do you not understand? We already had this conversation about Staccato in New York. I'm trying to get out of buying stolen product and smuggling it into the country. I got talked into it in the States by Sammy. I sure as hell don't want to get caught doing it in Canada, where I have a lot more at stake with my business and my family here. Enough of this craziness. Jesus! My friends are getting me into more trouble than the crooks!"

Frank sat back and folded his arms across his chest. He looked at Dale silently for a few moments. "You really are a shitty partner, Dale."

Dale glared back at him and said nothing.

Frank unfolded his arms and put his hands on the desk. "But you don't surprise me. I thought you might not want to work with my new business connection in Montreal. That's OK, we'll come up with something and I'll leave you out of it. You're not that good at this stuff, anyway."

"I don't want to get good at it," said Dale.

"In know. But, I do have another idea that you might like better."

"Dammit, Frank, can't you just let it go?"

"But I've gotta make a living too, Dale. Honest buck or not. And I have expensive tastes. I've had enough of your cheap restaurants and bad food."

He stood and stretched, looking out the window, then back to Dale, "Your coffee's pretty good though." He sat down again in front of Dale's desk. "OK, now let's forget Montreal and get back to our friends in New Jersey and their plans for California," he said.

"Your friends," said Dale.

"Right, my friends. But I'd like to introduce them to your friends. Remember I told you the guy running Stack Distribution for Tony Staccato was Pat Cametti? He'd like to meet Sammy Wong. He thinks they could do business together. Maybe then we could just get out of the way. He'll even pay a generous finder's fee and I'll be equally generous and give you half. How's that for a plan, partner?"

Dale shrugged and threw up his hands again.

"I'll give you credit for persistence, Frank. But I don't want any of Staccato's dirty money. You can take me out to one of your fancy restaurants with it, instead. I'm OK with helping you spend the dirty money." He smiled at his own version of playing by the rules, then added, "But aren't you forgetting? Sammy also wants to get out of the smuggling business."

"I know, but I thought he was still trying to satisfy the Triads over there. Don't they still want a piece of him? He's probably helping them move stolen product, anyway."

Dale knew it was still a problem for Sammy. He had the impression Sammy was going to look after them by shipping to the Triads in California. *Maybe he could handle some shipments to the Mafia there, too. Better than using our joint venture in Boston.*

"I think you're right, Frank. Sammy's still on the hook with the Triads and he's probably shipping to them in California. But I'm not sure he's looking for more customers for stolen product."

"Well, let's see what he's willing to do. When can you talk to him again? We need to set up a meeting with Pat Cametti in the States. There's no way he's gonna stick his nose into Triad territory to visit Sammy in Taiwan. They have a bit of a war going on with the Triads, remember?"

"Yeah, I remember you starting that war."

"I didn't start it. Just threw a little gas on the fire."

Dale took a moment to consider the possibilities and how he might get the right people in place and extricate himself from the whole crooked operation. *Why the hell can't these gangsters stay on their own turf and leave the computer business alone? We have enough crooks in the business without them.*

He crossed his arms and leaned back in his chair. "Sammy usually comes to COMDEX every November," Dale said.

"It's the big international computer show in Las Vegas every year. I'll find out if he's coming this year and maybe they can meet there. Las Vegas is a popular spot for the Mafia too, I'm told. You should come as well and make sure the arrangements work for everybody. Besides, I'll be there to give you a tour of COMDEX and you'll learn even more about the computer business. Maybe develop some better business opportunities and a new career plan."

"Dale, you need to stop worrying about my career plan. I've got everything under control. But, I've never been to Vegas and I hear it's a hot spot for entertainment with lots of great restaurants. Maybe I can buy you dinner there, when we do this deal."

"Let's not get too far ahead of ourselves. I can't speak for Sammy and he may not want any more to do with these guys either."

"I thought you told me he was an ambitious businessman who didn't mind playing outside the rules. Hasn't he already dragged you offside a few times?"

"Yeah, that's Sammy, alright. He's willing to bend the rules, much farther than I would. But what he likes, even better than making money, is spending it on gambling, girls and booze. Especially in Vegas. That's where he gets in more trouble of a different kind."

"Sounds like my kinda guy. So let's meet him in Vegas. Maybe we can both work on you a little and get you into more trouble, too. Which do you prefer? Gambling, girls or booze?"

"I don't need your help, Frank. I'm in enough trouble already with Sammy and his Triad gangster friends. COMDEX is all business for me. Lots of meetings with my old business partners from Toronto, our current suppliers and the new ones I'd like to do business with. It's a lot to squeeze in over a few long days and short nights. No time for trouble or even the entertainment. No girls or gambling and not much booze, but thanks for offering."

Again, Frank was not surprised.

Dale continued. "The hotels and casinos in Vegas actually complain about the COMDEX crowds. There's over a hundred thousand computer geeks and engineering nerds there for a week every November and they still don't spend enough on gambling, girls and booze to satisfy them. So they'll be glad to see you, Frank. You'll help to get their numbers up."

"Vegas is sounding better all the time," said Frank. "Just don't count on me wandering around any computer shows."

"You and Sammy will definitely get along," said Dale. Now, let's call it a day and go home. I'll make plans tomorrow for you to meet Sammy at COMDEX."

19.

The annual COMDEX exhibition and conference for computer dealers and manufacturers started in Las Vegas in 1979. Over the years, it expanded to separate annual events in Chicago and Atlanta, but Vegas was always the biggest and the best, not only because of the attractions of the Strip, but also because of the proximity to the major computer product manufacturers and software developers in Silicon Valley, south of San Francisco.

COMDEX also attracted all the second tier manufacturers from Japan, Korea, Taiwan and China. The manufacturers from China did not become important to the computer industry until later in the 1990s, but they were quietly building their expertise domestically and doing their competitive research at COMDEX with everyone else. COMDEX was a high energy event that occupied the city for a full week each November, driven by the incessant search for innovative new products delivering higher performance and lower costs to the market.

Dale was in the dining room of Caesar's Palace for his meeting with Sammy Wong. He sat alone in a large red leather booth that was large enough to seat eight. The same dining room had been the scene of their prior meetings at COMDEX and the large booth assured more privacy for their conversation, away from the industry buzz around them.

Two years earlier at COMDEX, Dale and Sammy had agreed on their joint venture plans for Boston. Dale had initially presented the idea to Sammy, while he was grumbling about losing more than a hundred grand in a bad run of cards at the Caesar's Palace Casino. Dale had persuaded him that investing in 3D Computers was a much safer bet.

He saw Sammy approaching from across the room. His brisk stride and wide smile suggested today had been a good day at the tables.

*He looks very pleased with himself, energetic and sharply dressed for the evening. Must have plans after our dinner meeting. Probably a haircut first, Taiwan style. I'm sure he has lots of choices here to meet his needs.*During one of Dale's early visits to Taiwan, Sammy had introduced him to his barbershop routine.

"Time for a haircut, Dale," he said. "It'll help you relax and recover from jet lag." Dale soon discovered there was not usually a haircut involved. They went into Sammy's barbershop in Taipei and Sammy led the way past the barber chairs down a dimly lit hallway to private rooms at the back. In a small reception area, they were met by scantily clad young ladies, anxious to look after them for a pleasant afternoon.

Dale came to accept Sammy's recommended treatment after the physically draining long-distance flights to Taiwan, but he declined the "full service" massage that Sammy enjoyed so much in the adjacent room.

Sammy stepped up into Dale's booth and slid over to shake his hand. "Hey, Dale, here we are again at COMDEX. How was your day?" He settled onto the smooth leather bench seat and reached for the glass of water beside his place mat.

"Great to see you here again, Sammy," said Dale. "It's a good for both of us. I get an update on what's new and you get into a little trouble, far from home."

He smiled at the memories of Sammy's bad influence and his own careful sidestepping of any behaviour that would have been unacceptable to Susan.

Dale was never tempted, but often amused, occasionally disgusted, by some of the other businessmen who took advantage of the opportunities to misbehave while they were far from home and lost in the crowd. The stories didn't always stay in Vegas and sometimes followed them back home to make trouble there.

"It was a long day today, Sammy, with lots to see. It gets a little nuts at the major exhibit halls. Everybody's loud and obnoxious, trying to get attention for the latest product that's going to be the next big winner. They've got music and lights and entertainers in the booths, all trying to persuade the visitors going by to come in and listen to their sales pitch."

The computer exposition was more subdued in the early years, but the growing size and number of competitors forced hard sales tactics on everyone to avoid getting ignored.

"You might enjoy the booth-babes there, Sammy. Lots of tall blondes in short skirts with big boobs, standing in the booths and drawing a crowd. Maybe it's worth a trip over there for you."

Sammy smiled. "Thanks Dale, but I've already made arrangements for my own babes."

"OK. I'm sure you'll be well looked after in Vegas. Just don't include me this time, please."

Dale signaled for a waiter to come to their table. "Let's order dinner, then we can talk a little business, before you take off and enjoy your babes for the rest of the evening. How about our old favourite, steak and lobster? It's my treat, since you always look after me so well in Taiwan."

"That's good for me," said Sammy. "Thanks for being the host in Vegas. I'm not sure when I'll see you again in Montreal or Boston."

"Yeah, I realize that. So let's talk about Montreal and Boston, first. Then I have a new proposition for you. Maybe we can solve some of your other problems in Taiwan."

Sammy looked intrigued, but decided to wait for Dale to explain.

The waiter came over and Dale ordered for each of them a medium-rare steak and a broiled half lobster. He selected a bottle of French wine and the waiter left them alone.

"We're still going gangbusters in Montreal, as you can tell by the increasing orders and the accelerated shipment schedule on Chung-Wai. I hope you can keep up," said Dale. He paused and waited for a reply.

"We'll look after you all right. Don't worry."

"Good, I'm counting on you, Sammy. Since we cut off the lying, cheating assholes at KCS in Korea, you're the only supplier I've got for EXL monitors. It's never a good idea to be single-sourced, as you know, but we're partners now, so I hope I'm getting priority treatment."

"Of course, Dale. Remember, I did try to warn you about KCS. You should have stayed with us from the start. But now I'm happy to help you kick their ass. How are we doing in Boston?"

"That's going great, too. We're still getting up to speed, but the staff are all working hard and sales are growing. You'll see the orders increasing for Boston soon, too."

"That's great, I think we can drink to that."

The waiter had filled their glasses, after Dale tasted the wine and nodded his approval. They clinked glasses and made a toast to their continued good fortune. Sammy appreciated a good wine, too. Neither of them were going to drink any of the cheap California stuff that flowed in tanker truck quantities at the discount buffets that were so popular in the hotels and casinos on the Strip. The cheap food and drink kept the customers in place, throwing their money non-stop into the slot machines that were conveniently located everywhere.

"Business is good, Sammy. But I know you still have some problems with the Triads in Taiwan, so I have something new for you to think about. Maybe it'll work for you, I don't know."

Sammy looked confused and a bit concerned. He gripped the large steak knife in his small right hand and carved a pink slice of steak into bite-sized pieces. He waited for Dale to continue. "This is another deal with my friend, Frank, remember I told you about him when we were in Taiwan?"

"Your friend who set up the disaster in New Jersey?"

"Well the disaster wasn't really part of his plan, but yeah, he's the guy. They call him Frank the Fixer and I call on him whenever I need to deal with criminals. He helped me get away from the Montreal gangsters a year or so ago, before I ever asked you to rescue me from the loan sharks."

"Didn't he also introduce you to those loan sharks?"

"That's right. He has some dangerous friends in different places, but sometimes they're the only way out. He's not thirty yet, but very tough and resourceful. He can be dirty and violent if he needs to be, but I trust him more than anybody I've ever worked with. He's in Vegas with me this week and I'd like you to meet him tomorrow. I think you'll like him, too."

"Sounds like quite a guy, Dale. I'm happy to meet him, but what does he want to propose? Not more illegal shipments, I hope."

"Well, he may be able to help you out, actually. Are you still getting pushed around by the Triads and your fat friend, See Yeung?"

Sammy looked nervously around the room. "Careful Dale, those guys are everywhere. Certainly in California, probably here too. There's lots of Italian Mafia in Las Vegas and the Chinese Triads follow them everywhere. They're like swarms of wasps, all attacking the same picnic basket."

"You're right and it's no picnic for anybody," said Dale. He pushed their empty plates and utensils toward the centre of the table, leaning closer to Sammy and speaking more quietly. "How are you doing, keeping See Yeung happy?"

"He's never happy," replied Sammy. "He's squeezing me for twenty thousand a month now and still trying to push me to smuggle more stolen product into the States through our warehouse in California, this time. I keep stalling because we're not making that many shipments there."

"Well, maybe that's where we can help. You remember Tony Di Staccato and his guys from New York who ripped off the Triads in New Jersey? Well, he's looking for more product now on the West Coast. They were happy with the ATI video cards that you shipped to them last month but like See Yeung and the Triads, they're never satisfied. Frank has been talking to them and he'd like to introduce you to the guy who runs Stack Distribution for Tony Di Staccato. His name is Pat Cametti and he's in Las Vegas this week, too."

"Sounds like you've got it all organized for me, Dale."

"I'm not pushing anything, Sammy. I know you're going to make your own decisions, but I promised Frank I would set up a meeting. You two will get along fine, I'm sure."

Sammy sat back in the booth and contemplated the challenges they had dealing with the Triads and the Mafia. "OK, Dale, I'll take a chance on you and Frank. Let's meet here again tomorrow, same time and place. No time for dessert tonight, though. I have another meeting." His cheerful face split in a wide smile. "See you tomorrow."

Sammy slid out of the booth and walked quickly out of the dining room toward the lobby. He looked even smaller than usual, surrounded by over-sized marble statues of Roman Emperors along the wide hallway leading to Caesar's Casino.

Dale looked at the unfinished bottle of wine and decided it was too soon to call it a night. *I'm in the entertainment capital of the world, after all. Maybe there's a good show to see tonight.*

Siegfried and Roy are still a big draw, especially after one of their performing white tigers tried to kill one of them. Maybe this new Cirque de Soleil everyone's talking about? Apparently, it was originally a bunch of street buskers, clowns and musicians from Montreal. Now it's a global sensation. No man-eating tigers, but trapeze artists and gymnasts from around the world. They're at Treasure Island, just down the Strip. Maybe more interesting than dessert.

He decided to ask the waiter for both a dessert menu and a brochure on the shows for the week.

20.

As Dale expected, Sammy and Frank enjoyed meeting each other at dinner the next night. The three of them sat at the same booth again.

Frank dwarfed Sammy beside him, but his large frame sprawled across the bench seat helped to fill the space for eight. The two men started by exchanging stories, immediately after they had been introduced.

Sammy asked about Somalia. Frank had not been back since he had escaped at seventeen, but he had some horrifying tales of the violence there, ending in tragedy for his family. Dale had not heard all the stories before, himself.

The large African young man and the tiny middle-aged Taiwanese gentleman quickly established personal rapport over their common upbringing in poor families and the difficult circumstances of their third-world homelands. Frank did not say much about the actual killing of his parents. He was still too affected by it. He was more forthcoming and obviously proud of how he'd been able to rescue his sister from Somalia and continue to look out for her in Montreal.

They all laughed together over a few of the stories of his arrival in Montreal. The French Canadian kids in the first neighbourhood where he lived were fascinated by his blackness and his Muslim religion and impressed by his skill on the soccer field. He had some challenges with the local bullies and street gang leaders, until he demonstrated the tough ruthlessness he had learned from his experiences in Somalia.

Montreal street violence was pretty mild by comparison. Sammy listened intently and then related some of his own history, growing up in the hills outside of Taipei. Life was tough for his family too.

"Between the poor years and the shortages during the war, we learned to survive, eating rats and snakes and squirrels, anything with a bit of meat on it. That's why those foods are still popular today, although the vendors now try to push them as rare delicacies. It's all in the sales pitch, right Dale?"

Dale was starting to think his own comfortable, peaceful childhood in the beautiful Rocky Mountains of Western Canada had been too easy. *Maybe I'd be smarter, tougher and more resourceful too, if I'd grown up in circumstances similar to Frank and Sammy. But I'll never know and I'm not going to feel guilty about it.*

Sammy continued his own story. "Things started to get better for us after the Cultural Revolution in China during the '60s. They left us alone a little more in Taiwan. That's when we discovered that capitalism and free enterprise work a lot better than Communism, to bring people out of poverty."

He sat back and spread his arms wide over the table full of delightful food and wine, turned to take in the whole elegant dining room of Caesar's Palace, then raised both fists over his head, in triumph.

"And look at us now!"

They all laughed together, then settled down to enjoy their dinner, each distracted by his own thoughts flowing from the conversation. After a few quiet minutes, the dinner conversation flowed back to the less weighty subjects of Las Vegas celebrities and the shows they'd all enjoyed the previous evening.

As they cleaned up the remnants of beef and shellfish on their plates, Dale interjected. "OK, gentlemen, enough of the friendly chit-chat, let's get back to our reason for being here."

Sammy looked at him sharply. "You're no fun Dale, forget about that. It's time for entertainment again, right?"

Frank laughed. "You're right Sammy, Dale's no fun. He's always worrying about his business and pushing too hard to make more money. He needs to relax and enjoy life a little."

"Don't worry about me, Sammy," said Dale. "I'm OK with less excitement and quietly making a few bucks the old-fashioned way. Frank's in a big hurry and he doesn't mind if it's a little shady. I usually say, 'No thanks,' to his wild ideas. He has some shady ideas for you now, Sammy, and you might decide, 'No thanks' too. But I'm stepping aside and leaving you to it. For now, my priority is dessert. Let's take a look."

Sammy took the menu from Dale, but looked at Frank to continue. Frank ignored the dessert menu and picked up the cue. "It's great to get to know you, Sammy. Dale always says good things about you and now I know for myself."

He pushed his empty plate aside and leaned forward with his elbows on the table to continue.

"As Dale said, I wanted to talk to you about a request from the guys at Stack Distribution in New Jersey. They're giving us a hard time over the single shipment from Taiwan and they want us to do more. I don't want them to get any more persuasive than they've been so far. That could get very nasty. Maybe not as nasty as the Triad gangs you have to go home to, but they could make life miserable for all of us. I'd rather have them on our side. Not just because they pay well, but because I'd rather have them in front of me and not be looking over my shoulder for them."

"Dale explained all that," said Sammy as he nodded in agreement. "I'm not sure which gang of thieves is worse. These guys you're talking to were pretty violent with the job they did on the Triads in New Jersey."

"Yeah. I know that gave you a problem with your guy in Taiwan," said Frank. "And I also know they don't want to do business with our Italian friends in America. So we'll have to muddy the water a little to put this together.

"I'm thinking if you take the stolen product from the Triads in Taiwan and pay them what they want, they won't care what you do with it. We'll have to mark it up some for Staccato, like we did with the ATI cards, then we can all make a buck in the process."

He looked to Dale for anything to add. Dale gestured for him to continue.

"Dale doesn't want to be part of this new arrangement. Last of the good boy scouts. I think he's hoping to become a Christian missionary somewhere, but I dunno."

He grinned at Dale, who shook his head and scowled back at him. He had nothing to add.

Frank turned to Sammy. "That's a good thing for us, he'll cost us less. Dale always wants to make a buck on these deals, if he gets involved."

"So do I," said Sammy.

"See, Frank," said Dale. "Sammy and I agree. You're the partner who's hard to get along with."

"Wait'll you meet Pat Cametti," said Frank. "See how easy he is to get along with."

Dale started to get out of the booth.

"I'll let you guys carry on and decide which bunch of gangsters are worse. I'm trying to avoid them all and get back to my boring business." He tossed the dessert menu back on the table.

"No dessert for me, either," he said. "I have another meeting tomorrow morning, so I'll see you at breakfast, as usual, Frank. You can give me a recap of your meeting with Cametti. Good luck with your new friends, Sammy. Please don't sign me up for any more deals with the Triads or the Mafia."

"OK, Dale," said Sammy. "We'll keep all the fun to ourselves." He didn't look convinced that Frank would be introducing him to more fun this evening.

Dale left them together in the booth and headed to the exit from the dining room.

21.

Later that evening, Frank and Sammy were in the reception area of the Stardust Hotel and Casino down the Strip from Caesar's palace, waiting to meet with Pat Cametti.

"Just ask for Dino Mancini at the reception desk, when you get there," Cametti had told Frank on the phone, when they had spoken about arranging a meeting with Sammy Wong. "He'll set up a meeting room for us."

Frank and Sammy were not waiting for long. A slim, dark-tanned man with slicked-back brown hair, dressed in a sleek grey suit with felt-lined lapels, wearing a high-collared white shirt and bright yellow silk tie, approached them from a hallway ending beside the front desk.

"Good evening, gentlemen, I'm Dino Mancini," he said, reaching out to shake hands. "Welcome to our little pleasure palace in Vegas." He smiled, exposing brilliant, too perfect to be natural, white teeth. "I hope you're taking some time to enjoy Sin City. Not working too hard, I hope."

"It's quite a place," said Frank. "You really do know how to make a business out of doing pleasure. And I'm sure it's a pleasure doing business here, too."

"It's my favourite place to mix business and pleasure," added Sammy.

"Glad to hear it," said Dino. "But I understand you're here to do business with my old friend, Pat Cametti. He's waiting for you. Please, follow me."

Mancini turned from the reception area and led them past the elevators, down a wide brightly lit hallway and turned right into a wood-panelled corridor with closed double doors on both sides. The large overhead sign at the entrance to the corridor stated Conference Rooms. Mancini stopped beside the first double doors on the right, with a plaque indicating the Sierra Salon. He knocked twice and then held the door open for Dale and Sammy to enter.

In the small conference room, they saw Pat Cametti, seated at the far end of a broad oval table. To his right, sat his associate, Dominic Santaguini. Against the far wall were two more men. Frank recognized Carlo from Stack Distribution, seated with a new sidekick, a bulked-up body builder with scrawled blue tattoos on the back of his hands. There was no sign of Pauli with the broken nose.

On the table was a bottle of red wine and in front of Pat Cametti and Dominic Santaguini were two full glasses. Six empty wine glasses sat on coasters around the perimeter of the conference table. In the centre was a chrome tray with a plate of biscotti and napkins stacked neatly beside it. On a second chrome tray was a large thermos of coffee, six white coffee cups, a bowl of sugar and a small pitcher of cream.

The two men at the conference table rose and Frank and Sammy reached across the table to shake hands. Dino Mancini introduced the four men, ignoring the two bodyguards against the wall. Frank and Sammy sat on one side to Pat Cametti's left, opposite Dominic Santaguini.

"Please, gentlemen, help yourself," said Dino Mancini, gesturing to the two trays on the table. "I'll be back a little later." He went out the door and left them alone.

"Good to see you again, Frank," said Cametti, "and it's my pleasure to finally meet the highly recommended, Mr. Sammy Wong."

Sammy smiled and nodded acknowledgement.

"I gave Sammy some background, Pat, on your business at Stack Distribution," said Frank. "Maybe you can explain your plans in California. Sammy might be able to supply you there better than we could in New Jersey."

Pat Cametti nodded briefly and looked at Sammy.

"You know we're not a regular distributor, though, right Sammy? We specialize in quick turnaround of high value product and we want it at prices that can't be beat. We sell at a premium and do pretty well for everybody. We'll make it worth the trouble, if you can deliver what we need. You manufacture computer monitors, I know, and you ship regularly to California. We're not interested in the monitors, but I understand you have some very good connections in Taiwan and you can get us product at the prices we need."

"Yes, I do have very good connections in Taiwan, and in Hong Kong and America. They're not all in the Triads, by the way. We might be able to find some product for you, but our connections are not all that keen on shipping to …"

He was interrupted by a tap, tap at the door and it opened again to Dino Mancini. Mancini entered the room again, this time with two strangers behind him, both heavy set Chinese men in dark suits. They came in and stood beside him.

Cametti turned and growled at Mancini. "Dino, who the fuck is this you're bringing into my meeting?"

Dino stepped aside and indicated the men standing beside him.

"This is Kim Phat from L.A.," he said, "and his brother, Sung Phat. They asked me to introduce you, when they heard you were coming to Vegas and planning to do business in California."

"This is a private meeting," said Cametti, looking at the two Chinese and wondering how they knew so much. "You're not invited."

"Well," said Kim Phat with a smile at Cametti, "going where you're not invited is exactly what I wanted to talk to you about."

He took a seat at the opposite end of the conference table and indicated the chair to his right for his brother. Sung Phat sat down beside Frank and they casually sized each other up.

Kim Phat looked at Pat Cametti and placed his folded hands on the table. He looked around at the others, making eye contact with Frank and Sammy, glancing quickly at Dominic Santaguini and the two body guards.

"Let me explain," he said.

Dino Mancini stood by the door, hands clasped behind his back and looking intently at Kim Phat, avoiding the angry glare of Pat Cametti.

Kim Phat continued. "We're part of a group in L.A. with very good friends in Taiwan and Hong Kong. Maybe you've heard of the Chinese Triads, or the Bamboo Union in Taiwan. It's our version of your Italian Mafia, same kind of family business."

He smiled at Sammy Wong. "Your friend, See Yeung, says hello, Mr. Wong. He wants me to remind you, we do not do business outside the family. We will not supply product to you for your new Italian friends."

He turned back to face Pat Cametti at the other end of the table.

"You see Mr. Cametti, we have an understanding in California with your Mafia friends. We share territory and don't interfere with each other's businesses. We both have enough trouble already with those renegade maniacs, the Hell's Angels. We don't need to go pissing in each other's beds, too. Part of our understanding is that you stay out of the computer business in California. Even in Vegas we get along without fighting, right Dino,"

"That's right," said Dino, stepping forward to the table and looking now at Cametti.

"We work to keep the peace here in Vegas too, Pat. We don't need any more attention than we already get from the Feds. I figured you should meet these guys, so you can understand how it works and how it keeps us all doing good business without fighting over territory.

In Vegas, they leave us alone with the casinos and the hookers, we stay out of the drug business and the protection racket."

"So basically," interjected Kim Phat, "you're not welcome in the computer business on the West Coast. Just like we're not welcome on the East Coast. It's better for us all to respect territories and keep the peace."

He stood up and his brother rose beside him. He scanned the table again, resting his eyes briefly on Frank, Sammy Wong and Dominic Santaguini, before speaking directly again to Pat Cametti.

"I wanted to let you know, myself. California is not a good place for Stack Distribution. We've already got it covered. So don't waste your time here, trying to set up supply with Sammy Wong and his friend, or anyone else. Just relax and enjoy Vegas. I'm sure Dino will take good care of you, before you fly home."

He started for the door, but an angry Pat Cametti stood quickly, his armchair rolling back to bump against the wall beside Carlo, who rose simultaneously and reached inside his suit jacket to rest his hand on the gun handle protruding from his shoulder holster.

"Just a second, asshole," said Pat. "Nobody tells us where we do business or who we do business with. Especially not the Triads. We know how to look after you, just ask your friends back in Jersey."

Kim Phat nodded slowly and smiled again.

"Not my friends and not so smart, these guys in Jersey. You were right to push back on them," he said. "But before you declare war on us out here, I suggest you talk to Dino. He'll explain how a war costs us both some good soldiers and accomplishes nothing, except bring more heat down on us all. I recommend a peaceful solution. You stay where you are and so do we."

He turned to Dino. "Tell him about the casino owner, who wanted to get into the drug trade. We had to torch his house here in Vegas." He led his brother to the door and turned back to add, "His wife and kids were still in it."

They left and the door closed behind them.

Pat Cametti clenched his jaw and stared at the closed door for a few seconds, then reached for his chair, pulled it back to the table and sat down again. Carlo removed his hand from the gun handle and turned to sit down again beside the other bodyguard.

Dino Mancini took the seat vacated by Kim Phat and waited for Cametti to say more. Frank and Sammy looked back and forth between the two men at each end of the table, waiting for the first to speak.

"OK," said Cametti, "it seems we have some complications here." He looked at Frank and Sammy.

"You guys don't seem to have much of a plan, either," he said. "How about you both go back to your hotel. I've got some shit to sort out here with Dino. I'll call you in the morning, Frank."

As Frank and Sammy left and walked back down the corridor, they heard, through the closed Sierra Salon conference room doors, the sound of a chair crashing violently against a wall and Pat Cametti shouting.

"What the fuck did you set me up for here, Dino? I didn't come for the good time. You knew that!"

They couldn't hear the mumbled response from Mancini, as they walked on and out through the casino.

22

The next morning, Dale walked downstairs from his room on the eighth floor at Caesar's Palace to his breakfast meeting with Bobby Brydon of BIG Technology Products. BIG was another small computer products distributor in Montreal, but they specialized in storage products – floppy disc drives, hard drives and tape back-up, while Dale's 3D Computer Products specialized in display products – computer monitors, video cards and related accessories.

The two business owners had met years ago, when Dale was still at AES Data, and they had kept in touch to occasionally compare notes and commiserate over the challenges of computer products distribution and the brutal competition they both faced in their small independent businesses.

They were under constant pressure from the big multinationals with their comprehensive product lines and huge marketing budgets and from the smaller new importer/distributors with their predatory tactics, all of them aggressively trying to steal customers from each other.

In Montreal, Dale and Bobby met most often for breakfast or lunch at Benny's on Fifty-Fifth Avenue in Dorval, which was conveniently close to both their offices. At their last meeting, Bobby had introduced a new proposition.

"You know Dale, we'd both be better off if we put our businesses together into one powerhouse distributor. It would be a great strategic fit for our complementary product lines without any conflict in suppliers or customers or territory. We'd increase our combined sales and reduce our combined costs. It'd be a helluva bottom line. You're not opposed to making more money, are you?"

Dale had already been thinking he needed to get bigger and expand his product lines for his business to continue to thrive.

"I agree, it makes a lot of sense," said Dale. "But we'd have to work on how to put our two businesses together. We've both had a few years now running our businesses alone. It'll be a big challenge to go back into a partnership with shared ownership. We both know that can make everything more complicated."

"But we both know what mistakes to avoid," said Brydon. "It's just a matter of defining roles and responsibilities up front, then respecting and trusting each other enough not to interfere with the other guy's job. I already know you're a better manager than me and I'm better at sales. So that's a good start."

Dale silently accepted the compliment on his management success, but he disagreed with Brydon's assessment of his better salesmanship. He'd heard rumours from some unhappy customers that Bobby had a habit of making big promises, then failing to deliver. His business reputation was suffering for it. Dale worried about it.

I don't need to add to you to my own business challenges and I certainly don't want to risk our reputation in the market. We know how to quickly fix our own mistakes, but I don't want to have to start cleaning up for yours. That's a big negative for me.

"Listen, Bobby, a merger of our businesses has great potential for growth and for defense against all these new competitors. Bigger is better. So, let's keep working on it and we'll see where it goes."

They had agreed to follow-up in Vegas, where Dale could do some research on the data storage business, since all the latest products and the biggest manufacturers would be installed in the exhibits at COMDEX.

Brydon continued to push his merger proposal over breakfast at Caesar's. "It's time we introduced you to the real heart of the computer business in Silicon Valley, Dale. That's where all the big name manufacturers are. You must have had enough of those low-ball imitators in Korea and Taiwan by now".

Dale was silently agreeing with him. *He has a good point there. Probably fewer surprises and detours into illegal shit, too, working with the major players in Silicon Valley.*

"I think you're right, Bobby, I need to know more about storage products and look at diversifying and expanding our product lines. I'll spend some more time with Micropolis and Seagate, maybe some of the other big names, while I'm here. We can follow-up when we're both back in Montreal and decide what to do next."

Brydon was keen to follow up, as soon as possible. "Before the end of November, OK?"

Dale was left with the impression that Brydon was in more trouble than he wanted to admit and needed a strong business partner soon, before his problems went beyond his ability to recover. *You're not doing so well and fading fast. Maybe I can do better. I just might learn enough here to become your worst nightmare, instead of your new partner.*

Dale had finished his breakfast meeting with Brydon and was enjoying one more coffee, while planning his tour of the major manufacturers and learning about their new data storage products. He was making notes in the COMDEX exhibit directory, when Frank walked through the dining room up to his table and pulled out a chair.

"Hi, Frank," said Dale, "I just finished my meeting. How'd it go for you guys with Cametti?" *He looks in pretty good shape. Maybe they didn't get into a long, hard night of carousing in Vegas after their meeting with Cametti.*

"Well, it didn't quite go as planned," said Frank. "We had some unexpected guests show up from the Triads in L.A."

"Oh, shit," said Dale. "That doesn't sound good. Not another gunfight between the Mafia and the Triads, I hope."

"I thought we might see guns blazing at one point, but this guy from California, named Kim Phat, was pretty convincing without pulling out any weapons. Kind of a diplomatic representative for the Triads, I think. Violence was threatened, but not necessary. We were 'shaken, but not stirred.' This time, at least." He poured himself a coffee.

Dale waited for him to say more.

Frank continued. "Anyway, it's the end of the story for Sammy shipping stolen product to Cametti and Stack Distribution in California. Sammy may still have to deliver for the Triads, who probably won't let go of him yet, but Cametti called me this morning to say 'no deal' for him. He's flying back to New York today. Let's just say, he decided the computer business out here is not that interesting."

"That's odd," said Dale, "I just spent the morning with a new potential partner, who thinks there's lots of good business to be done out here. Maybe I'll be expanding to California myself."

"If you stay clear of the Triads and the Mafia, you might be all right."

"Oh, yeah. They were never part of the plan, as you know."

"So, it's all good for you, Dale, but dammit, I'm looking for work again."

Dale reached for the coffee thermos on the table, topped up Frank's cup and filled his own. "Time to take a deep breath and smell the coffee, Frank. See if you can find work that's legal and doesn't involve the Triads or the Mafia. I'm sure you could handle a safe, boring job, where nobody's threatening to take a shot at you."

"Haven't found anything that appeals to me yet, Dale. Let me know if you find something."

"You're on your own, Frank. I can't keep looking after you, anymore. I've got to tend to my own business."

"What? I thought you still wanted me to take good care of you."

"Yeah, well I hope I don't have to call on you anymore. Let's try to keep it safe and boring for both of us."

Dale's train of thought took a new turn. "Speaking of taking care of me and my family, are you still keeping an eye on Boncanno for me?"

Frank shrugged and swallowed a mouthful of coffee. His manner turned serious. "Ah, good old Gino Boncanno. He's not up to much, it seems. Still lying low and trying not to attract too much attention. He's not worrying about us, I don't think. He wants to be sure the cops and the Renaldi family leave him alone, whatever he's doing. I've asked around, though, and it seems he's getting organised for a comeback. Maybe he's ready to forgive and forget what we did to him, but I doubt it."

"That's not very comforting, Frank. Sounds like he should've been put out of business permanently."

"That was the plan, but he's a tough, miserable sonofabitch. Like us, Dale."

He sat back in his chair and saw that Dale was not relieved by the facetious comment.

"Keep an eye on him, Frank. Maybe we'll have to shut him down again ourselves, before he comes after us again."

"Maybe. I'll check on him when I get back to Montreal."

"I'm nervous for my family, Frank. They're not going to be safe if Gino is back in business and still holding a grudge against me."

23.

Back at home in Montreal, it was a bright sunny Friday and unusually warm for mid-November. Warm enough for Susan to be wearing a light track suit over her tennis outfit. She looked very smart, young and athletic, in dark blue with thin white piping down the sleeves and pant legs, her short brown pony tail bouncing at the back of her light blue peaked cap.

She strode quickly from the Provigo grocery store toward her Camry station wagon in the parking lot with two bulging green and red shopping bags swinging from her hands.

She was having a productive morning. Got the kids up and organized early, drove them to school and had a brief meeting with Sean's teacher to talk about his interest in joining the Computer Club in the next grade. Then she went to meet her girlfriends at the Lakeshore Tennis Club. She'd been there for a couple of hours of team practice with the coach and afterwards had enjoyed lunch with her teammates.

On the way home, she stopped at Provigo to pick up a few groceries for the weekend. She was expecting Dale home from Las Vegas late that evening and she was counting on him to be ready for dining out on Saturday night with their friends, Ron and Pattie Anderson.

She was looking forward to the evening. *I'll have to call and book the babysitter for tomorrow night. I wonder what I should wear. Dale will be distracted, as usual, I'll have to get his attention with something sexy. Maybe that dark blue dress with the short skirt, he likes. With the pink La Senza panties and bra that I like.*

When she got home, she would change into something more practical and sober for her afternoon visit to the palliative care centre where she volunteered for a few hours a week.

She packed her groceries into the rear of the Camry beside her tennis bag and got into the driver's seat. She pulled out of the parking space and turned left towards the exit and home.

Susan didn't notice the dark blue sedan parked across the lane in the lot a few spaces over. A tall, long-haired man was watching her through the tinted windshield.

She was not aware that he had followed her, earlier that morning, from home to the school and then to the tennis club, too.

*****

REMEMBERING MOM

"So, what fantasy world are you working in now, Sean?"

"It's not a fantasy world, Dad, it's a likely future world. Where we're all fighting robots, to keep them from taking over."

"Wow, sounds fascinating," said Dale. He shook his head slowly in disgust. "They actually pay you to play computer games all day?"

"Yeah, that's what I do, play all day." Sean returned Dale's look of disgust. They were meeting for lunch at the Second Cup coffee shop in Old Montreal, not far from where Sean worked at UbiSoft.

"You're such a dinosaur, Dad. Hard to believe you used to work in the computer industry yourself. Yes, they actually pay me pretty well to play with computer games all day. Almost what I'm worth. And with a PhD in computer science and engineering, I can design games like nobody's seen before and manage a team of a hundred-and-thirty software developers to build them. We've built some of the best-selling games in the market."

"Yeah, but they're still games. Why not work on something more important with all that education and talent, like building a colony on Mars or stopping global warming."

"Well, we don't have a plan for Mars in Canada's space program and I don't think I can write software to solve global warming. Maybe I could help them with their predictive modelling, though. They use a lot of high-end artificial intelligence and simulation applications that were developed first by the gaming industry. Actually, a lot of the most advanced industrial applications were developed by the gaming and entertainment industry. That's the big attraction for computer geeks like me. We're really at the leading edge with a lot of the technology."

"That sounds familiar, actually. Even when this old dinosaur was selling hardware back in the 80s and computer games were just getting started. They were already using a lot of leading edge technology in computer graphics and high-definition displays. I didn't understand the appeal of computer games then and I still don't, but apparently it's grown into a multi-billion dollar industry, bigger than the movie business."

Sean nodded. "Yup. Globally, the industry is worth over seventy billion a year and growing faster than any other sector of the entertainment business. A lot of the technology we develop for games spills over into other more productive uses, as you call it. So, I think I'm contributing something of value to society. Even though it's primarily entertainment, gaming may be doing more for public health and education than it gets credit for."

Dale went quiet and looked thoughtful. "I know, Sean. Your Mom would be proud of you."

Sean had been a bit agitated. He was suddenly more subdued as he looked at the sadness on his father's face.

"I miss her too, Dad."

He reached across the table and squeezed Dale's arm. Dale looked up at his son.

"She died too young, dammit. She should still be here."

=======

Part 3.
Settling Accounts

24.

Monday morning after the trip to COMDEX, Dale was seated at the small round conference table in the corner of his office, shuffling through computer print-outs.

At 3D Computer Products, Dale's private office was at the back of an open area that stretched along a row of windows facing the street. At the front was the reception desk, where Marie de Carlo welcomed any visitors and directed all the incoming phone calls. There were closed offices along the wall and across the aisle against the windows the desks were separated by low partitions.

Across the street and running down the block on both sides were more of the same flat-roofed, light industrial buildings with exteriors in brick and aluminum and wide paved parking lots in front. Warehouse access from the street was by a lane that ran along the back of the units.

Dale paused over the computer print-outs and glanced at the pile of brochures and product specifications that he had brought back from COMDEX. He leaned back in his chair to gaze out the window into the grey sky. His mind was on Susan and the kids.

Are they really safe?

I'm carrying on at work as if all's well and they're probably doing the same at home. Kids at school, Susan running around all day with her volunteer work, her tennis and the kids' commitments. But I know she's still worrying.

Maybe I should get a mobile phone installed in her car. It might be useful, in case of emergency. But they're not cheap, over fifteen hundred dollars installed. She's not that much in her car, anyway. Maybe one of those new Motorola portables. She'd hate that, though, big ugly electronic brick stuck in her purse.

His thoughts were interrupted as the phone on his desk buzzed and he heard Marie de Carlo over the intercom.

"Dale, I have Jim Annapoulis from ABJ Data on line two for you."

"OK, I've got it."

He pushed away from the conference table and went to his desk, looking at the flashing line on hold. He wondered if this was another problem he didn't need.

Dale knew Jim Annapoulis and he knew his company, ABJ Data Products, as a strong competitor in the computer product distribution business. They had met several times before at computer events in Toronto.

Annapoulis had started his company a few years before Dale and it had grown to be one of the biggest and most successful in Canada, competing very successfully against the three big multinationals all based in the U.S – Ingram, Merisel and Tech Data.

Jim was the eldest of three brothers who ran the business and he was clearly the leader in achieving their successful growth.

ABJ Data had a well-developed strategy of selecting products with high profit margins and limited distribution in Canada, then building the market and taking control to protect their profit margins. ABJ Data even had access to some Apple and Dell Computer products that were not normally available through the distribution channel.

Dale suspected that Jim Annapoulis might have a complaint. Dale had been responsible for persuading Patrick Jensen, his Sales Manager, to leave ABJ Data and join 3D Computers. Maybe that was what this call was about. He picked up the line.

"Hello, Jim, how are you? It's been a while."

"I'm in Montreal this week, Dale, and I'd like to meet you before I go back to Toronto Wednesday evening. I think we're missing an opportunity to do business together and I'd like to discuss it."

Quick to the point, thought Dale. He knew Annapoulis had a reputation for skipping the social niceties.

"Sure," said Dale. "We can meet at the end of the day Wednesday before your flight, if you like. How about the Airport Hilton Bar about four thirty, five o'clock?"

"Good, see you there at five." Click, and he was gone.

*****

At the Hilton on Wednesday, Dale and Jim Annapoulis were seated at a low table beside the wall, as far away as possible from the noisy customers crowded around the large U-shaped bar in the middle of the room. Dale silently cursed himself for making such a bad choice of meeting place at the end of a week day near the airport. They had to lean forward over the table to hear each other and keep the conversation private.

Annapoulis was clearly uncomfortable with the forced intimacy, but again got to the point quickly, after a sip of his scotch.

"Dale, I know you're doing well here in Quebec and I hear good things from Patrick Jensen. He thinks you're a good manager and sees you growing the business quickly. I think I should buy you out, before it gets too expensive."

Whoa! That was not expected. Dale reached for a small handful of peanuts from the bowl on the table. He held them in his hand and replied, "Well, thank you, Jim, we are doing pretty well. Sorry about taking Patrick from your Montreal office, by the way. He's been very good for us and I'm sure you were sorry to see him go. I hope he hasn't told you too much, but he's very honest and has high integrity, especially for an ambitious sales guy. And just so you know, he never offered and I never asked for any of your customer lists or other confidential information." He tossed the handful of nuts into his mouth and reached for his glass.

"No problem," said Annapoulis. "Slavery's not legal in Canada, so people can leave whenever they want. Patrick's a good guy and I trust him, too. I'm sure he's doing well for you, without doing us any harm. Besides, I'll get him back if I buy your company. What do you think?"

"Well, I actually hadn't thought about it at all, before now." *But maybe this is the exit I need to get away from all my problems.*

Especially the gangsters, like Boncanno, who'll never leave me alone. Maybe it's time to call it quits, like Susan suggested. Maybe not. He did say the price would be better, if I keep on growing and I'm not done yet.

"I'm not sure how that would work, Jim. What did you have in mind?"

"Well, we've done a few other acquisitions and we have a process that works well for everybody. Essentially, we agree on a price, make a deal on the terms and the future role of the current owner, then merge the business with ours. We'd want you to stay on, probably give you national responsibility and more product lines to manage."

"What about Boston? I have a joint venture there with a partner from Taiwan. And what about my EXL product line? I have partners in Toronto and we share territories in Canada."

"We don't have any U.S. operations and I don't want to poke the bear in the U.S. Those guys already give me enough grief in Canada, so you'd have to sell the Boston business to your partner. In Toronto, we could make a deal to respect the current territories and maybe add EXL to our existing product lines."

"But I'd be an employee, not a shareholder in ABJ Data."

"All our current shareholders have the same last name," said Annapoulis. "So, yes. It's family only and I have control with the majority of shares. That doesn't change with new acquisitions. But you get to realize the cash value of your equity in 3D Computers immediately and still maintain your high personal income. It's good for you, Dale. Struggling to succeed in your own small business is very risky. Especially in today's market. If you don't join the big guys, you're going to get crushed by them and lose everything. This gives you a quick and easy exit at a good price."

He sat back and sipped his scotch, watching Dale think about his proposition.

He makes a pretty persuasive case, thought Dale. *Hard to deny the risks of continuing alone.*

"It's an intriguing proposal, Jim. I'm flattered by the offer and appreciate the opportunity to consider it. But, I really don't think it fits my current plan to grow the business and keep control myself."

Dale sat back in his chair and sipped his scotch. Then he leaned forward to continue. "I bought out my original partners a couple of years ago, so I could keep my independence. Before starting 3D Computers, I had a bad experience at AES Data where somebody else was managing my future and that convinced me to never let that happen again. Maybe I'm stubborn, or stupid even, but I'm not ready to sell yet."

"I see," said Annapoulis. "I didn't know you were at AES Data. I was there too, right after I graduated from engineering. I learned some hard lessons and I don't intend to repeat the mistakes AES made. A good company, but they failed to transition from word-processing to the personal computer world and they've been going downhill ever since. We're actually going to reach their best sales number of two-hundred- million-a-year at ABJ in the next two or three years. Maybe sooner, if you join us. It's up to you."

"Let me think about it some more, Jim. I'll get back to you next week, if that's OK," said Dale.

Jim pushed his glass back across the table and ignored the bar bill that was slipped into an embossed Airport Hilton folder. "Thanks for the drink. Call me next week then."

He picked up the small carry-on canvas bag and the black Targus laptop computer case beside his chair. He shook Dale's hand and headed for the door to take the shuttle to the airport.

Dale watched him leave. *I wonder what my business is worth right now. Over two million? Maybe more? More is better, so let's get back to work and avoid any more distractions. This little motivational meeting with Annapoulis was definitely worth it.*

Dale reached for the bar bill and pulled his wallet out of a back pocket. His mind was running through calculations of the value of his business.

Let's see, if I take the annual bottom line and use a multiple of five times, maybe seven times, we're worth, maybe ....

Jeez! Fifteen dollars for two scotch and some peanuts? And he'll expect a tip on top of it.

He pulled a twenty-dollar bill from his wallet, put it in the Airport Hilton folder and held it aloft to call the waiter over to make change.

25.

On the other side of the city from the airport in Dorval, Frank the Fixer was on his way to a meeting with Paulo Renaldi at Ottimo Financial Services.

Renaldi's office was on Sherbrooke Street East, near the looming tower of the Olympic Stadium, a soaring monument to the mismanagement and corruption of the 1976 Olympic Games in Montreal. The infamous collapsible roof over the stadium had never functioned properly and was a source of constant taxpayer complaints about the ongoing maintenance costs. Neither the City of Montreal nor the Province of Quebec could ever find a mutually acceptable solution to avoid the financial burden that lasted for decades.

Mayor Jean Drapeau had famously declared that the Montreal Olympics could never lose money, any more than "a man could have a baby." He was reminded of that foolish remark for the rest of his life.

Mayor Drapeau attracted the international spotlight to Montreal with EXPO '67 and then the Olympics of 1976. But the financial debacle of the Olympics was the start of the economic decline of Montreal, accelerated by the ascension to power in the provincial government by the separatist Parti Québecois, that same year. Pride and patriotism exploited by manipulative politicians with visions of grandeur has a long history in Quebec.

Frank was oblivious to all the political history and symbolism as he parked on Sherbrooke Street in the shadow of the Olympic Tower. He looked back at the tower standing out against the sky between the downtown skyline and the profile of Mount Royal further west.

It was not Frank's first visit to the elegantly furnished offices of Ottimo in the modern brick and aluminum ten-storey office building. The quiet reception area and Paulo Renaldi's office with all the luxurious carpets and paintings gave Ottimo Financial Services the appearance of a private investment advisory firm. It was not.

Ottimo Finance had wealthy, largely anonymous investors in the business, most from the Renaldi family. But its clients were people in financial difficulty. They came to Ottimo when they couldn't get the money they needed from regular banking channels. Ottimo specialized in providing funds to those desperate for help and without access to more reasonable financial resources. The term 'loan sharks' accurately described their voracious lending practices and ruthless collection tactics.

Dale Hunter had been introduced to Ottimo and Paulo Renaldi by Frank the Fixer, when he had his own financial difficulties, two years earlier. Ottimo had offered financing and protection from Gino Boncanno. Then suddenly, Ottimo's demands for repayment became more than Dale could handle. In the end, he was only able to satisfy Ottimo when he received the five-hundred thousand dollars from Sammy Wong.

Frank was visiting Paulo Renaldi to bring him up to date on his meetings and the conclusions of Tony Di Staccato and Pat Cametti about doing business in California.

"Our planned meetings in Las Vegas didn't go so well," he explained to Paulo. "The Triads were pretty clear about staying away from their territory and the computer business out there. Pat Cametti's friends in Vegas and L.A. also told him they didn't want him disturbing the peace they've negotiated. Apparently the biker gangs, the Triads and the Italian families are avoiding open warfare by sticking to their agreed territories and they don't want any new players involved."

"Stack wouldn't back off for anybody, if he really wanted to be there," said Paulo. "That's never been part of his modus operandi. But he hates California, too damn hot and sunny all the time."

"Doesn't sound like a complaint to me," said Frank.

"Or anybody else in Montreal, this time of year," said Paulo with a flicker of a smile. "I think it's more about losing interest in the computer business. He wasn't ready to go to war over that."

"Not easy to make a buck in the computer business, apparently," said Frank. "Although our friend, Dale Hunter, still seems to be doing all right for himself."

"Good for him," said Renaldi, "but the rest of us can't keep up with the technology. It changes too damn fast. Yesterday's hot product, we could sell at any price. Next thing we know, it's obsolete and nobody wants it. I don't get it, the stuff still works OK and suddenly it's worthless."

"Like those laptops you see now for $3000," he continued, shaking his head in dismay. "Today they're worth stealing to make a quick buck. Next thing we know, they'll be down to $300 and not worth the trouble. Then it's just a useless smash-and-grab for petty cash, not a jewelry heist for big bucks, anymore. We're better off in the old trades we know we can count on, like drugs and gambling. They're never going away. And financing," he added, with another flicker of a smile. He pointed at the Ottimo Financial Services business cards on his desk.

"That's where we know what we're doing."

Frank had been nodding agreement during Renaldi's ramble. "You're right. Lucky Luciano came to the same conclusion last week. He's decided to stick to what he knows. But that means he doesn't have any work for me, so I'm not very busy these days, Paulo. Anything I can help you with?"

"Maybe, Frank. Let me think about it. My brother, Vito, he's looking at some big investments to, uh ... rollover, our surplus cash. He might be able to use you."

"OK, let me know when I can meet him and we'll see what I can do," said Frank.

"OK," said Paulo. "I'll talk to him and give you a call." They both pushed their cups back to the centre of the coffee table and stood to leave.

26.

That evening, Frank was sharing a sofa with Hélène Bourassa at her apartment in Laval, just north of Montreal. They were facing each other, fingers touching along the back of the sofa and knees touching on the cushions.

They were both relaxed and barefoot in the warm glow from the gas fireplace opposite the sofa. Frank was in tight-fitting blue jeans and a black tee-shirt. Hélène was bra-less in a pink knit V-neck hanging loosely over a pair of long white cotton shorts. Two glasses of Chardonnay sat within reach on the low coffee table in front of the sofa.

Through the wide eighth-floor window behind them the dark silhouettes of tall buildings were perforated by squares of yellow light from the apartment interiors.

"So, we have a problem," said Frank. "I'm bored and looking for work again,"

"You say that, Frank, but you never want to look for a real job. You prefer stick-handling between the good guys and the criminals to make a fast buck. Why don't you go legit and find something that lasts?"

Frank leaned back, stretched and looked up at the ceiling before replying. "You think I should be a cop, like you?"

"No. You're not cop material, you're not willing to play by the rules."

"There's no money in playing by the rules. The people in charge make the rules and they're the only ones making any money. Cops who break the rules to make a little on the side, they get caught and end up in jail with the same bad guys they put away. That's not what I'm looking for."

Hélène straightened her legs and crossed her bare feet under the coffee table.

"You just have to learn how to work without breaking the rules," she said. "Bending them a little is OK, but you have to avoid going too far."

"You mean like our friend, Pierre?"

Pierre Forsey was a detective who worked with Hélène at the Montreal Police Force. Forsey had a reputation for being on the payroll of some of the gangsters he was supposed to be pursuing. They both knew he had a long-standing arrangement with Gino Boncanno.

"I'm not talking about Forsey," said Hélène. "He keeps his job because he's careful and not greedy. Yes, he plays in the grey area and makes deals he shouldn't, but he brings in enough of the bad guys that the top dogs at the Station don't ask too many questions. Prosecutors don't either, but some of the defence lawyers may dig for dirt that Forsey doesn't want them to know about. That's where he's at the biggest risk of getting caught by one side or the other. Something you should be careful of too, Frank. You can't keep working both sides without getting caught in the crossfire at some point."

"Don't worry about me, Hélène. I have very good survival instincts. And I like working both sides, it keeps me sharp. I'm never gonna be a cop."

"I'm not suggesting you should be a cop, Frank." She paused and reached for a sip of wine, before sitting back to look at him again.

"But you need to stop being the Lone Ranger, riding in on a white horse to save the day. You don't even have a Tonto to watch your back."

Frank looked confused. "What are you talking about, Hélène?"

"Oh, sorry. I guess you didn't grow up watching the Lone Ranger on TV. He was a mysterious masked man, a cowboy on a white horse, saving innocent victims in the Old West. His Indian sidekick was called, Tonto. You never heard the background music 'dum-da-da-dum da-da-dum-dum-dum,' and 'Hi Ho, Silver! Away!'? His big white stallion was called Silver. It was a popular TV show when I was a kid."

"Are you kidding me? We never had TV in Somalia. And I never grew up idolizing cowboys. You're talking about a Hollywood hero. Good guys in white hats killing bad guys in black hats, right?"

"Yeah, the Lone Ranger was pretty much that old stereotype. But, at least he had a good Indian buddy, in Tonto."

"That's not the stereotype, I've heard about. Didn't those cowboys in the Old West say, 'The only good Indian is a dead Indian'?"

"Yeah, but that thinking's not acceptable any more. The old prejudices still exist, but I guess Tonto was an early Hollywood attempt to change the attitude and be a little more sensitive to the Indian point of view. I grew up with it, living next door to the Kahnawake Mohawk Reserve in Chateauguay, but we still have some of the old prejudices. People are slow to wake up.”

“So you know all about Indians, Hélène. Maybe you can be Tonto, if I’m the Lone Ranger.”

Hélène laughed. “Interesting idea, Frank, but we can’t work together, if you’re still on the wrong side of the law half the time. We need to get you straightened out. Since you’ll never be a cop, how about getting your licence as a P.I.”

“A what?”

“A Private Investigator. You know, like that guy, Magnum, on TV.”

“More TV heroes you want me to imitate?”

“No, I don’t want you to be a fake Hollywood hero. This is for real. You’d be like an independent cop, working for yourself. There are still some rules to follow to keep it legal, but you can take any client you want and do almost whatever you want, to solve their problems.”

“That sounds more like me.”

“Right, all you need to do is to take a course, pass the exam and get a licence. Then it’s ‘Hi Ho, Silver! Away!’ You can go riding off after the bandits and cattle rustlers, rescuing fair ladies while you’re at it. You should look into getting a P.I. licence and see if that works for you.”

Hélène moved off the sofa and reached for her wine glass. She raised it to Frank with a smile and winked. “That’s enough career counselling for tonight. Let’s relax and take care of our other needs. We’re both good at that.”

Frank smiled back at her and reached for his glass to clink it gently with hers. "Now there's a good idea. Let's get naked again and go back to bed, my fair lady."

Hélène put down her glass. She stood and opened her arms to Frank with a "Hi Ho, Silver!"

Frank got up and pulled her into his arms. Their mouths found each other, as she swung her legs up and wrapped them around his waist.

27.

It was an early winter day in the suburban neighbourhood where the Hunter family lived. The trees in the front yard were bare and the flower beds were empty beside the driveway where Susan had parked after returning home from the tennis club.

She was rushing from the laundry room, where she had just tossed her tennis bag, and was heading into the kitchen for a sports drink from the fridge. The doorbell rang.

She was in a hurry to change and meet her friend Francine for lunch, so she didn't check the window or the peep hole in the door to see who was there, before yanking it open.

She was startled to see a tall greasy-looking stranger standing close to the door. Looking past him, she saw a white minivan parked in the driveway. The engine was running and a driver was sitting in it.

"Mrs. Hunter," the man said.

"Yes?"

He stepped forward abruptly and pushed the door open, knocking Susan backwards.

"What the hell! Who are you?"

He closed the door behind him and snapped the deadbolt shut, then turned and grabbed her arm tightly with his left hand. His right hand came out of his jacket pocket and with a flick of his wrist, he was pointing a switchblade at her chest.

"Just shut up and do as you're told, you won't get hurt. Get into the kitchen," he said, pushing her down the hallway.

"We need to call your husband."

*****

Dale was at the office, catching up on developments in Montreal, since he had been away a lot the last few weeks. It was a Thursday morning and it seemed unusually calm at 3D Computer Products.

Maybe it was the pre-Christmas lull before the annual shopping frenzy when everybody would be buying gifts for the holidays. Computer products were on everyone's shopping list, especially home computers, laptops and software for computer games.

Dale had just returned to his desk from the service department and he was concerned about the backlog of monitors returned for repair that were piled high in the warehouse and taking longer than usual to fix and return to customers.

Product failures and defects were always an issue he needed to watch closely. It had been a serious problem in the past. The Korean manufacturer for EXL monitors, KCS, had decided to substitute a component to reduce costs, but it had been very unreliable and an unacceptably high percentage of those monitors had failed within the first few months of use.

Fortunately, Guy Tremblay had found the problem quickly and KCS had agreed to pay for the product recall and replacement of parts. Dale was hoping this was not another epidemic of product failures. He was looking at Guy's service reports when the phone buzzed on his desk and Marie at reception came over the intercom.

"Dale, I have Susan on line 3 for you."

He poked the button for line 3.

"Hi Susan, what's up?"

He heard a man's voice on the line that he didn't recognize. "Your wife can't come to the phone. But I need to talk to you."

"What? Who are you? What's going on?"

"Hang on, I'll let her explain."

He heard the man's muffled voice again, but couldn't hear what he was saying. Then Susan was on the line.

"Dale, for God's sake! I don't know what's going on. This guy has a knife on me. Ow-w-w! You fucking asshole!"

The man's voice came back on.

"You're wife needs to co-operate, Hunter, and so do you."

"What have you done to her? You hurt my wife, goddammit, I'll see you in Hell!"

"Relax man, just a little scratch to let you both know this is for real. Now listen up and we can sort this out."

"Let me talk to her."

He heard the man say, "Tell him you're OK." Then he heard Susan call out to him.

"It's OK, Dale, he just poked my arm a little. I'm fine. Talk to him and find out what's going on."

"There you go, Hunter. Listen to your wife and do as you're told, nobody gets hurt."

Dale clenched the phone tightly. He tried to breathe calmly and listen, as the man continued.

"Now, here's what's going to happen next," he said. "It's not complicated. I'm going to take your wife to a safe place where we'll keep her for a while. As soon as you deliver a hundred thousand in cash, we'll give her back to you."

"Are you crazy? I can't come up with a hundred thousand cash, just like that! Who the hell are you? Why are you after me and my wife?"

"Too many questions, Hunter. I'll call you in two hours and you better have some good answers for me by then. We won't wait long for the money, so get on with it!"

The line went dead.

Dale broke into a sweat and dropped the phone into its cradle. *I've got to get there before he leaves with her.*

He grabbed his keys and rushed out the door to his car. It was normally fifteen minutes to twenty minutes to his home from the office.

The BMW bumped roughly out of the parking lot and Dale drove frantically through the industrial park to the highway, terrifying a few other drivers on the way. He raced west on Autoroute 20 to Saint Charles Boulevard, then made a screeching exit north and turned right, into his neighbourhood. He slowed and cautiously approached the street where he lived, checking the oncoming traffic for any suspicious looking vehicles. They all looked suspicious.

As he drove up to the house, he saw Susan's blue Camry wagon in the driveway. He stopped beside it, ran up the steps to the front door and flung it open.

"Susan!"

There was not a sound, except the echo of his own voice and his hard breathing. He rushed upstairs calling her name again, knowing it was futile. He came back down into the kitchen and immediately saw the notepad on the countertop by the telephone. It had a message for him.

Hurry up Hunter!

There was a small red streak of blood on the corner of the note, where the switch blade had been wiped clean.

Dale slumped onto a stool at the kitchen counter and stared at the note. His stomach churned and his brain bounced in all directions. *I have to hurry.*

He got up and ran a cold glass of water at the sink, drinking it in one long swallow. He set the glass on the counter beside the note and tried to calm himself.

I thought I was done with gangsters and their threats of violence. It's been almost two years. Is it the same bastards again? Or somebody else?

There had been some home invasions in the neighbourhood and a story in the newspapers about a bank manager, whose wife was held captive at home while he was forced to cooperate during a robbery at the bank.

Why are they after me and holding my wife for ransom? It's gotta be that sonofabitch, Gino Boncanno, again. Frank said he'd never give up on getting revenge. He must be behind this. And that means he won't be satisfied with the ransom money. It's my hide he's after.

"You won't be safe 'till Gino's dead," Frank had said. "He has a long memory. Especially if he's not getting enough respect. And we really disrespected him, Dale, by not letting him kill you when he tried."

It might not end with delivering the cash, but I still have to come up with the hundred grand.

Dale rushed upstairs to his home office and quickly unlocked the desk drawer with the cash box in it. He flipped it open and grabbed the bundles of bills to count how much he had. *Twenty-three thousand, that's seventy-seven thousand short. Next stop is the bank. I need them to co-operate. Immediately. No questions asked.*

He went back out the front door, hesitating whether to lock it or not. He thought about the kids at school who would normally be brought home about three o'clock. Susan had arranged the car pool today with Pattie Anderson. She had taken all the kids to school, so Pattie would be bringing them home. *I'll have to call Pattie before she picks them up. What the hell do I tell her?*

He left the door unlocked and went to his car. It smelled hot from driving hard. Dale took another deep breath to calm himself and drive more cautiously, knowing his mind would not be on the road or the traffic. He called Frank from his car phone.

"Dammit Frank, call me back right away, this is an emergency."

Frank never answered his phone when it rang, but he was usually quick to call back. This time, Dale had just pulled into a parking space at the bank near his office when Frank called him back.

"I think that bastard Boncanno has kidnapped my wife," said Dale. "I'm at the bank now for the hundred grand they want to bring her back." He explained to Frank what had happened.

Frank agreed with him. "Sounds like Boncanno is back on your case, all right."

"I doubt if the hundred thousand is all he wants."

"You're probably right again, Dale. He wants your head, not just your cash."

"Well, I want my wife back, safe and sound. Then we can go after Boncanno. We need to stop him permanently this time, Frank."

"Alright, you go get the cash, in case we need it. I'll work on a plan to deal with Gino. I'll call you again, as soon as I have something."

28.

The Commercial Bank of Montreal had a branch on Fifty-Fifth Avenue, just two blocks from Dale's office.

Dale was not sure how well this sudden request for cash would fly with his long-time banker, Rick Petrie. He'd never made a hundred thousand dollar cash withdrawal before.

OK, let's say eighty thousand, just enough to add to the bundle in my briefcase. Dale went up to the cashier.

"Hello, Mr. Hunter, how may I help you today?"

OK, let's answer the question and see what happens. "Good afternoon, Marie-Claire." Her name tag helped. "I need to make a big payment in cash, so I need eighty thousand from my account, right away. Can I sign a cashier's check or something to get it quickly?"

"Oh." She looked taken aback, then reached for some forms stacked on the shelf above the counter in front of her. "Sure, if you'll just sign a withdrawal slip, I'll take it to Mr. Petrie for approval."

She filled in the form and handed it to Dale. He signed it and gave it back to her. She pushed her cash drawer shut, locked it and went down the hall with the paperwork to Petrie's office. After a few moments, he came back with her.

Rick Petrie was the local branch manager, who handled the accounts for 3D Computer Products. He had been helpful through some difficult periods for Dale and they had developed a mutual respect. Petrie came out beside the tellers' counter to greet Dale and shook his hand.

"Say, Dale, that's a lot of cash you need. Somebody won't accept a check instead?"

"Yeah, pretty old-fashioned, eh? Not a problem, is it?"

"No, if that's what you need, we'll give it to you. Just come down here into the back office, so we're not handing that much cash over the counter. Don't want anybody to think we're getting robbed."

He smiled, but Dale was not in the mood for friendly banter. They went into a small office beside the row of tellers. The cashier arrived with a tray of cash and counted out eighty thousand in bundles of five and ten thousand dollars, onto the desk in front of Dale. She handed him a small blue cloth bag with the bank logo on it and a receipt to sign.

Dale signed it, then dropped the cash bundles into the bag and stuffed it into his briefcase beside the fat brown envelope of cash from home.

"Everything OK, Dale?" asked Petrie. "Please be careful carrying all that cash around."

"Yeah, yeah, no problem. Not something I like to do either, but sometimes you gotta do what's necessary to make the deal. Thanks, Rick."

Dale stood and shook Petrie's hand. "Take care, bye for now."

*****

Dale quickly went back to his office and waited for the next call from the kidnappers. Frank had not called yet, either. Dale checked his watch and started calculating the timeline.

Let's see. The first call from the guy at home had been about eleven thirty. It's now nearly one o'clock. They said two hours. Where the hell is Frank?

Dale was pacing in his office and suddenly stopped. He went quickly around the desk and grabbed the phone. Flipping his Day-Timer open, he looked up a number and punched it in. A woman answered.

"Hi, Pattie, it's Dale. Glad I caught you at home. Listen, I just wanted to ask if you could keep Sean and Keira at your place this afternoon, until one of us can come by and pick them up later. Susie's not home for a while and I'm going to be home late myself."

He listened for a moment. "No, no problem. Just a little ... uh, change of plans. Anyway, one of us should be over there before dinner, so you don't have to feed them. I'll give you a call later, and let you know. Thanks a lot, Pattie, really appreciate it."

He put the phone down slowly. *Where the hell is Frank? And when is this bastard with Susan going to call?*

He slouched in his chair and stared out the window at the other businesses across the street in the industrial park. *I wonder how their day's going. Are the gangsters after them, too?*

He noticed the light flash on line one. It stopped, as Marie at reception picked it up. He glanced at his watch. It was 1:35. The intercom buzzed.

"Dale, some guy for you on line one. He says you're expecting his call."

"OK, I got it."

He jumped up from his desk and quickly closed the door to his office. He returned to the desk, sat down and picked up the phone.

"Hello?"

"Hunter, you got the money for us?"

Dale hesitated briefly, before replying. "Listen, dammit, I told you it wouldn't be easy to come up with a hundred thousand cash, that fast. I only have twenty-three thousand here, right now. I'm working with the bank to get the rest, but we need more time to arrange it. You gotta give me another couple of hours."

"I don't gotta give you nuthin'. You dumb sonofabitch, you negotiating a price on your wife?"

"No, dammit! I told you, I just need more time."

"I'll call back in an hour." The line went dead.

Dale dropped his head in his hands and leaned forward with his elbows on the desk. *What the hell am I doing? What if they don't call back and I never see her again?*

There was a tap at his closed office door and Frank opened it. He stepped in and closed the door behind him. He stood in front of Dale's desk and asked, "What's happened? Have you heard from them?"

"Where the hell have you been, Frank? I'm worried sick they're going to do something worse than kidnap my wife since I decided to stall and wait for you to come up with a better idea."

"Sorry, it took a while. It's all set up now. I'm ready to go after Gino. How much time do we have?"

"He said he'd call again in an hour, when I'm supposed to have the money."

"How come you don't have the money?"

"I do have the money! A hundred grand in cash, stuffed in my briefcase right there." He gestured to his brown leather briefcase, lying on the credenza behind him.

"But I thought we agreed. I shouldn't deliver it and walk into a trap until you had a plan to get us out of this bloody mess without anybody getting killed. Jesus, Frank, I'm working in the dark here, while some bastard with a knife is holding onto my wife."

"It's OK, we're all set. An hour should be enough for me to get Susan back to you."

"Really? What's your plan?"

"You don't want to know, Dale. I'll call you when it's done. I'm on my way to Gino before we stall any longer."

Frank turned and went to the door.

Dale stood. "Wait a minute," he said, but the door was closing behind Frank and he was gone.

Dale sat back down. More waiting and worrying was all he could do for now.

29.

When the men left the house with Susan, the tall one, who had come through the front door and poked her with the switchblade, pushed her into the back of the minivan.

"Get down in front of the seat. Stay out of sight and don't move. We're going for a ride."

Susan was shaking with fear and she looked away from him as she slipped to the floor. He got in behind her and placed one hand on her back to push her down. She crouched on all fours in front of the seat beside him.

The driver backed out slowly, then drove calmly away and down the street. Susan tried to keep track of the turns and the stops that she knew so well in the neighbourhood. She realized that they had gone north on St. Charles Boulevard and were now on Highway 40 going east across the north side of the city. After about thirty minutes, that felt much longer in her uncomfortable position, they left the highway on a long curving exit followed by more stops, turns and winding streets. She lost track of direction and distance.

After another ten minutes or so, they pulled up to a stop and she heard a garage door opening. The van pulled forward into the dark enclosed space and the door closed behind them.

"OK sweetheart, this is where you get out. Cover your eyes with this first."

She felt a piece of cloth drop on her back and pulled it over her shoulder. It was a stained white dish towel. She placed it over her eyes and flipped the two ends over her ears to tie at the back.

The man behind her grabbed it and roughly pulled it into a knot to hold it in place across the back of her head. She winced as it pinched her left ear, but didn't give him the satisfaction of releasing the stream of foul language that ran through her mind with the corresponding visions of violence she wanted him to suffer.

He opened the side door and helped her out. Her hands were not tied, so she felt her way forward to the cement-block wall of the garage. She stood straight and stretched the stiffness out of her back trying to get oriented. He grabbed her arm and pushed her towards a door in the corner that led upstairs. She shuffled blindly up the stairs, conscious of him following behind and too close to her short tennis skirt.

As she arrived at the top, she stumbled on the door sill and when she jerked her head up to avoid falling, the dish towel fell off her head. She was startled to find herself looking around a small living room with a kitchen and dining room to the right.

"Hey!" the man yelled. He yanked her toward an open door to the left, where she saw a single bed against the wall and a dresser below the window.

"Wait in here and don't do anything stupid."

He pushed her inside, tossed the towel in behind her onto the bed and closed the door.

Susie sat on the bed and looked around the room. She took a Kleenex from her pocket and wiped away the blood from the small wound on her forearm.

What the hell's happening here? What's Dale going to do? Are these the same gangsters who came after him a couple of years ago? They threatened me and the kids then, too. The kids! They'll be home from school soon and nobody's home.

She checked her wrist watch. The time was 12:45.

These guys are awfully casual about letting me see their faces. No blindfold anymore. Why are they not worried about being identified? Are they going to kill me before this is over? Dale too? A hundred thousand doesn't seem like a lot for ransom. They must have more in mind. They said they'd give Dale two hours to come up with the money.

The time passed. It seemed like hours, and her thoughts meandered. She wasn't sure if she'd heard them make the call. They'd been talking, maybe they'd called Dale already.

More time went by. She stretched out on the bed and tried to relax. She was too agitated to relax. She got up and paced the room. She stopped to listen at the door, but heard nothing. She remained alert while lying or sitting on the bed or pacing in the room. Her mind raced.

What happens next? Why is Dale taking so long?

*****

She heard the phone ring in the next room. She looked at her watch again. Now it read 2:20.

Someone answered and she could hear their voices. She got up and put her ear to the door, but still could not make out what was being said.

After the call, there seemed to be angry words between the two men in the other room.

Something's wrong. What's Dale done?

30.

Gino Boncanno had spent the morning at the Restaurant Vida da Vinci and was sitting at a small table outside the door of his office, enjoying a cappuccino with the *Journal de Montreal* newspaper spread out in front of him. His two bodyguards, Mario and Luigi, were stationed at another table near the front door.

Mario had his suit jacket draped over the chair beside him and was sitting with his sleeves rolled up, enjoying a big bowl of pasta. His partner, Luigi was patiently watching him and the front door, while sipping his own cup of espresso. The small cup in his big hand looked absurd as he picked it up pinching the tiny handle between his fleshy fat thumb and forefinger, crooking his little finger primly. He looked up from his coffee as a middle-aged Italian matron came in and walked past them toward Gino.

Gino nodded at her as she came in and walked straight to his table. She kissed him on the top of his bald dome and sat down with an affectionate smile. Gino frowned at the personal interruption while he was doing business, but then he relaxed and smiled back.

"How was your meeting at school, this morning?" he asked.

Gino had previously gone with his wife to the parent-teacher meetings at Saint Ignatius Catholic School for boys, but he and Maria had agreed that he should not go to any more meetings with Antonio's teachers. Gino had little patience with their polite mumblings about his boy and he had great difficulty restraining himself, if he thought they were not treating him well. It was better for everyone if he stayed away and let Maria bring him the news.

"Well, they say he's very shy," said Maria, "but well behaved and doing pretty well, except for French and the Morality and Religion classes."

Gino scowled. "His French is very good, better than his Italian. He uses it all the time with his friends in the neighbourhood. I'll teach him all the morality and religion he needs to know."

"Well, they say he uses too much street French and sounds like a *Québécois*, not the good French. His religion class is more history than religion, so you'll still have to teach him how to be a good Catholic. But some good news. Antonio is very happy to be in the band and playing the trumpet!"

Gino's eyes wrinkled with the smile of a proud papa. "Ah, good," he said. "Maybe we'll need to add sound proofing to his room, then." He continued smiling and patted his wife's hand, as she got up to leave.

Gino waved goodbye as she went out the door and he lifted his coffee cup to drain the remains. He wiped his mouth on the large white napkin, straightened his suit jacket and tie and left the dining room to go back into his office.

About a half hour later, another visitor arrived at Vida da Vinci. Gino was relaxing at his desk in the office at the back of the restaurant, looking at the English newspaper, *The Gazette,* waiting for news from Pietro Lombardi. There was a knock and the door was opened by Mario, who had his suit jacket back on. "There's a guy here, named Frank, says he needs to see you."

Gino frowned and thought for a moment.

"Big, black guy?"

"Yeah, tall, young. Big black guy."

Boncanno remembered this guy named Frank, called himself Frank the Fixer. *He's the trouble maker who saved Dale Hunter from my plans for him last time. He's also the one who warned me about the Renaldis. He'd been right about that. I think he also had something to do with it. What the hell does he want now?*

"Check he's not packing."

"I did, he's clean," said Mario.

"OK, send him in and wait outside the door."

In a moment, Frank filled his doorway. Wide shoulders, tall muscular frame in a tight denim shirt under a thin leather jacket, blue jeans that hugged his strong thighs and slim waist.

Tough guy, thought Gino, *maybe he's here looking for work.*

"Hello, Gino," said Frank. He turned and nodded at Mario, then closed the door.

Gino looked at him blandly.

"Mr. Frank, what can I do for you?"

He noticed something made of blue cloth in Frank's hand.

Frank held it up as he stepped forward and Gino recognized it as a small blue blazer with his son's Saint Ignatius school crest on the pocket.

Frank tossed it on the desk and said, "Young Antonio is safe for now. But I can bring you a piece of him, if you're not convinced we're holding him until you return Dale Hunter's wife."

Gino clasped his hands together and rested them on the desk in front of him. He pushed the blazer aside and squinted at Frank.

"I don't know what you're talking about."

Frank shook his head slowly and shrugged.

"OK, what piece of him would you like? A finger or the whole hand? Maybe a bigger slice? You want him cut up Somalian style or Sicilian?"

Gino's Face darkened. "You do not seem to realize you're making a very dangerous enemy, if you ever touch my boy."

"I already have lots of dangerous enemies, Gino. One more's no problem."

He came forward and leaned over the desk closer to Gino, who straightened in his chair to back away from him. Frank continued.

"I know exactly how important family is. But you need to know that Hunter is a part of *my* family and I'm very protective of him and *his* family. Did you think because the Renaldis aren't after you anymore, you could go after him? Big mistake, Gino. I thought you knew better."

He watched Gino unfold his hands and tap his fingers on the desk as he looked up at Frank.

"I know nothing of Mr. Hunter and what's happening to his wife. You need to talk to somebody else, I think."

"Gino, I am going to hurt your boy before the end of the day, unless you stop this and get Hunter his wife back. You need to a make a call, before I leave."

He sat down in front of Gino's desk, looked at him and waited. They stared at each other. Gino's eyes went to the closed door, then back to Frank.

After about a full minute of staring at each other, Gino reached into his breast pocket and took out a small leather notebook. He opened it and held his fingers on the page as he reached for his phone and dialed the number.

Frank heard someone answer and Gino quickly responded. "You can let her go," he said. "I've made other arrangements."

Gino listened to a loud reply on the phone, then interjected. "Yes, I know that. They won't go to the police, it's part of the deal."

He glanced up at Frank, who made no indication of consent. They stared at each other again.

"Call me back when it's done." Gino said. He listened to the voice on the line, then yelled into the phone.

"I don't want any argument, just do it!"

There was another pause as Gino listened. He added, "Yes, I'm at the restaurant," and hung up.

Frank leaned onto the desk and put his face close to Gino's. He slowly emphasized every word.

"If you ever come close to Hunter or his family again, if I even get a smell of you thinking about it, I'll take a piece out of *you* next time Gino, not your kid. It'll be a big piece and you won't survive to play these games anymore."

Gino squinted at him with a flame in his eyes that would have killed, if it were possible.

Frank went to the office door and opened it as Mario stepped back out of his way. Frank turned back to Gino.

"You'll get your boy back at school, as soon as I know Mrs. Hunter is home, safe and sound. Make sure that happens soon."

He walked through the restaurant, nodding to Mario and Luigi, and went out the front door to the street.

Gino sat silently, glowering at the open office door. Suddenly, he rolled out of his chair and shuffled quickly to the door. He looked out and saw that Frank had left the restaurant. He gestured to the two bodyguards.

"Come here!"

They both jumped forward and came to Gino, who was leaning on the door frame and looking past them to the street in front of the restaurant.

"Follow that black bastard," he said. "He's got my boy."

Gino turned back into the office and slammed the door behind him. He went to his desk and reached for the phone. He called the same number he had punched in earlier.

Gino's two bodyguards rushed to the front door of the Vida da Vinci and stopped there to look down the street for Frank. They saw him walking down the sidewalk to the right. He stepped between the parked cars and got into the driver's seat of a black Caddy, where he disappeared behind the dark-tinted windows.

Mario turned to his partner, Luigi and said, "Louie, get the car, bring it around front." he said.

Louie went out, hurried to the left and down the lane along the side of the building to the parking lot in back. A few seconds later, he drove a dark blue Pontiac sedan up the lane to the street and parked across the sidewalk where he could see his partner in the doorway.

31.

Dale was waiting in his office. Time was passing very slowly. He couldn't sit still. He paced back and forth in front of his desk. The door was closed again.

Frank had called him a few minutes earlier from his car.

"OK, Dale, I think we're getting there," he said. "I had my little meeting with Boncanno and persuaded him to let Susan go. You should hear from her soon, unless Gino decides to do something stupid. He's an evil, crazy man, so you never know."

"Jesus, Frank, that's not very reassuring. How the hell can I relax, if that's all you've got?"

"Hang in there, Dale. Call me back as soon as you hear anything."

The time continued to pass slowly. It was now after two o'clock. Dale wondered if he should go home. Maybe Susan would be returned there and the kids would be finished school soon. But everybody was calling him at the office. He had to wait there.

He sat and fiddled with the items on his desk. He glanced at the lights on his phone, they were all off. A passing thought that business was slow today, but he quickly deflected it to focus on Susan's kidnapping.

What's next? Dammit, this waiting and not knowing what's going on, it's killing me.

He clenched his fists and got up from behind his desk. He stopped staring at the phone and looked at the briefcase, still lying flat on the credenza, stuffed with cash.

He turned and paced back and forth across the room. He stopped at the book shelf along the wall and straightened the row of textbooks and business best-sellers, so the edges were perfectly aligned and precisely one inch from the front edge.

As he turned back towards the small round conference table in the corner, he saw the light flashing on line one. He reached for it, before Marie at reception could pick it up.

Maybe it's Susan!

"Hello?"

"You have the cash, Hunter?" He heard the same man's voice again. Dale shook his head with a start. This was not supposed to be happening. *Was this what Frank meant by Boncanno doing something stupid? Now what?*

"Yes, I've got it all now," he said.

"Good. Now listen carefully, this is what you're gonna do next. Get in your sporty BMW with the cash and leave right now. Don't call anybody, don't do anything else before you leave. Got it so far?"

Dale remembered Frank telling him to call, as soon as he knew anything. *Should I take the chance and make the call?*

"Yeah, I got it. Where am I going?"

"OK," the voice continued, "You're gonna drive into the city to Park Lafontaine on the north side and park on Rachel Street facing east. You know where that is?"

"Yeah, but Rachel is one-way west."

"Not at the park it's not. Just get there quickly, find a parking space and pay for the maximum two hours. Then leave the keys and the cash in your car. We'll be watching you. Just do it, walk away and go home."

"Jesus, you're stealing my car now, too? When do I get my wife back? I'm not walking away, until I see her safe and sound and you leave her with me. That's the deal. You got it?"

"You're fucking nuts, Hunter. You still think you're negotiating, here? Just do as you're told and you'll get your wife back. Maybe not the car, now that you mention it."

Dale clenched his jaw and took a long breath.

"I'm on my way. But I'm waiting in the car until you show me my wife." He hung up immediately to prevent any argument from the kidnapper.

He sat back and exhaled slowly. After a moment, he got up and put his briefcase on the desk blotter beside the phone. He drummed his fingers on top of it, as he thought about the instructions he'd just received. His stomach churned and he wondered what they were doing with Susan, or what they might have done to her already.

What should I do next?

32.

Mario was still standing in the doorway of the Vida da Vinci watching Frank in the Caddy and Louie was still parked in the Pontiac across the sidewalk. Nothing was happening. Mario looked toward Louie, raised his hands and shrugged.

He turned back to watch the Cadillac. *What the hell?*

Frank was walking down the sidewalk towards the restaurant.

Mario ducked inside and turned his back to the window, sitting on the sill and trying to look nonchalant. Louie slowly backed the Pontiac off the sidewalk and stopped back in the lane, out of sight.

Frank came in the door and turned to Mario.

"I'm not going anywhere. I'm waiting in my car for a phone call to let me know Gino's taking good care of his kid. He's a good Papa, right? You think he needs a reminder?"

Mario sat on the sill and looked blankly back at Frank. He said nothing. Frank turned and walked straight through the restaurant between the tables to Gino's office.

Mario quickly stood up from the window sill and started to reach for his gun, but Frank still looked unarmed with his bare hands exposed. Mario watched him continue past the wary diners. They were also watching Frank.

Frank threw the office door open. It banged hard off the wall and bounced back at him, as he caught the handle. He walked over to Gino, leaving the door open for Mario to watch the proceedings.

Gino looked up, shocked to see Frank again in front of him. "Now what do you want?"

"Is she free yet, Gino? I'm waiting for the call."

"Uh, I don't know. I told them. Maybe they already left with her to meet Hunter for the money."

"Not for the money, Gino. We're trading her for your kid."

"But when I called it was too late, they already made arrangements to meet with Hunter."

"Get on the phone and fix it now!"

"They're not there!"

Frank looked hard at Gino.

"OK, now I'll have to fix it myself. But you're coming with me."

"No!" Gino suddenly reached forward and pulled the desk drawer open for his revolver.

Frank was too fast. He took one long step around the desk, placed his hand on Gino's chest and pushed him backwards off the chair.

Mario rushed through the restaurant to point his gun through the doorway, but Frank had already yanked Gino to his feet and was holding the gun from the drawer to the side of his head.

Frank said to Mario, "Step aside, we're going for a drive."

Gino was flushed and breathing hard, wide-eyed and glaring at Mario. They both hesitated, considering their options, until Gino gave a slight nod. Mario stepped into the room and put his gun back in its holster.

Frank lowered his gun and poked Gino in the back with the muzzle. "Let's go."

They went past Mario and into the restaurant. The two tables of panicked diners were staring at them coming out of the office. They sat absolutely still and kept their hands in front of them on the table. Most knew this restaurant had ties to organized crime, but they had never been witness to an incident before.

Louie was standing near the door with one hand held close to his holster, but Mario waved him aside. He dropped his hand and stepped out of the way.

Frank held Gino's shoulder and pushed the gun into his back. He walked closely behind him down the sidewalk to his Caddy.

"Get in," he said, opening the front passenger door. Frank got in the other side behind the wheel and dropped the revolver into the side pocket of the driver's door.

"I don't know where we're going," said Gino.

"I do," said Frank, "I already talked to Hunter."

33.

Susan was in the bedroom at the holdout, getting tired and hungry. The emotional stress and fear were draining. She sat on the edge of the bed and wiped a tear that had slid to her cheek.

What the hell is happening? It's taking too long for Dale to get me out of here.

She heard the phone ring again in the next room and the voices were raised in an argument. The tall guy was yelling at somebody. She barely made out what he was saying, then heard the words get louder.

"Gino, she knows who we are! Dammit, we're better off if she's dead!"

The angry call continued, but she couldn't make out much more. She was sure it was still about what to do with her. Someone was pacing and judging by the long strides, it was the tall one. It was quiet again, then she heard them discussing something, but couldn't make out the words.

Shortly after, there was a knock at the door to her room and it opened a crack. She couldn't see him, but she heard his voice again.

"OK, lady, your time is up. We're going for another ride. First you need to pull a pillowcase over your head and use it like a blindfold. Forget the towel. Then back up to the door and I'll tie your hands behind your back, before we leave."

"Where are we going? What's happening?" said Susan. "Did my husband pay the ransom?"

"Shut-up with the questions! Just get moving and do as you're told."

Susan looked around the room. She had already checked the window. It was sealed shut and too late now to break it and climb out. She looked at the bed and reached for a pillow to pull off the pale green pillowcase. It looked clean enough.

She pulled it over her head and was momentarily dizzy, as she twisted it around her neck. She regained her balance and breathed slowly. Backing up toward the door, she puffed the pillowcase away from her mouth.

"OK, I'm ready."

The door opened and he grabbed her wrists and wrapped a cord around them to secure her hands behind her back. He held her arm tightly enough to hurt her, but she refused to complain. He pushed her back to the basement door and led her down the stairs.

She worried he might be tempted to push her violently down the steps, but she cautiously moved forward and he seemed to be helping her get to the bottom safely. Back in the garage, he opened the side door of the minivan and pushed her forward.

"Get in, you know the drill."

It was awkward with her hands tied behind her back and she banged a shin getting in, but she managed to crawl in and crouch on her knees leaning against the seat. The tall one got in beside her and pushed her ass with his foot, to give himself more space.

You bastard, she thought, *I hope you hang for this someday.*

The driver got in and she heard the garage door open. They backed out and drove away. She tried to focus on the turns and stops, but gave up, thinking she had no idea where they started from, so what was the point? She worried more about what the destination might be and what they were going to do with her when they got there.

It was not a comfortable ride. It lasted twenty or thirty minutes, but did not seem to be on any main highways. She heard the voice that she despised speak again.

"This'll do, pull in at the end, close to the grass."

The van came to a stop and the man pulled Susan up so she was facing him, still with the pillowcase over her head and her hands tied. He continued louder, close to her face.

"Now listen, bitch. This is important, if you want to survive. After today's little incident, you will forget everybody you've seen, everyplace you've been and everything that's happened today. You and your husband will never, ever go to the police. If the police come after us, ever, we will come after you again and you will not go home alive, next time. You got all that?"

Susan was still on her knees in front of the rear seat. She turned toward his voice.

"I've got it."

He shrieked at her, "Louder!"

She yelled back at him, spitting the pillowcase out of her mouth. "Yes, I've got it!"

He pushed her back down and snarled, "OK, now we're going to meet your loving husband."

The van pulled forward again. It rolled slowly along the side of Lafontaine Park, then turned east on Rachel Street.

34.

Dale had parked on Rachel Street as instructed, facing east on the north side of the park.

I'm not of getting out of this car until they show up with Susan. Not even to pay for the parking space. Shit! I don't need a cop standing here giving me a parking ticket when they show up.

He reached into the centre console for change to put in the parking meter. He took out a handful of coins and quickly got out to stuff the meter, then sat back in the driver's seat. He scanned up and down the street and checked the parked cars for any sign of the kidnappers.

The prick was right about the one-way street. Now, where the hell is he?

The two-lane section running east started at the corner of the park and continued past where he was parked. Dale watched and waited.

He noticed a white minivan approaching in his left side mirror. It slowed and stopped beside him. Dale looked at it and saw a woman's face pushed up against the glass in the rear passenger side window.

It's Susan!

He grabbed for the door handle to jump out. As the van jerked forward and accelerated away, he yelled after it.

"Hey, Susan! Wait!"

He started his car to go after them.

The van was already half a block away as Dale pulled out of the parking space. They were almost at the next intersection ahead, when suddenly, a black Caddy pulled out from the right side of the street and cut in front of the minivan. The van screeched to a halt and skidded left with a bang into a parked car. Traffic on the street came to a stop all around them.

Dale drove up behind the van and jumped out of his car. He slowed to approach the van cautiously from the rear. The dazed driver was leaning on the steering wheel and staring ahead at the Caddy stopped sideways in the street in front of them.

Frank was on the passenger side of the Caddy and leaning over the hood, holding the revolver to Gino Boncanno's head. He pushed Gino around his car toward the van, holding Gino's arm wrenched behind his back.

The rear side-door of the van opened and Pietro Lombardi stepped out. "Hey, Gino," he said, "looks like you screwed up. This was not part of your plan."

Gino glared at him, grimacing at the tight grip Frank had on the arm behind his back. His tie was twisted tighter than usual and his bulging face was bright red, instead of its usual healthy brown.

"I hope you've taken good care of Mrs. Hunter," said Frank to Lombardi. "Now give her back to her husband."

Dale took a few steps forward to the van as Pietro stepped away. Dale looked in on Susan, still huddled in front of the rear seat, apparently unharmed by the crash and waiting to find out what was going on. She was leaning cautiously towards the door, her head still covered by the green pillowcase.

Dale reached for her.

"Hey Susie, I've got you now. It's over, let's get out of here."

He helped her out and pulled off the pillowcase. He held her shoulders to look at her, then kissed her hard on the mouth. He hugged her tight for a brief moment, then quickly untied the cords around her wrists.

They ran holding hands back to his car.

Dale backed away from the van, then did a hard U-turn to drive west on Rachel, away from the crash scene. He slowed at the first intersection and glancing left down the street, he saw the flashing lights of an approaching police car, coming up beside the park. They were not ready to explain any of this to the police and they continued on west to go over Mount Royal and back home to the West Island.

Back at the accident scene, Frank growled in Gino's ear, before pushing him away towards the van.

"I'll leave you to deal with the police, Gino. Remember what I told you. Next time, I won't be looking for your boy."

ALONE IN THE WOODS

Dale stopped walking in the forest and looked up at the fork in the trail ahead of him. *Where the hell am I?*

He was standing on the mulched wood section of the trail and the wooden boardwalk ahead of him branched off, left and right, over the wet bog and through the trees. Dale had been lost in thought, walking through the quiet urban park and suddenly, for a moment, he was lost in the woods. He paused, got oriented again, then took the left fork to continue through the woods and around the lake.

Dale lived in a modern luxurious high-rise condo building on Nun's Island with a spectacular view of the city skyline and the slopes of Mount Royal behind it. He often went out for a solitary walk in the neighbourhood. Fresh air and exercise were his preferred escape from boredom to get re-energized.

This afternoon he had been at home organizing old family photos and converting the prints and 35-milimetre Kodak slides into digital photo albums for easier sharing with his kids. The photos had caused him to dwell on some beautiful memories of Susan, but looking back had left him sad and in need of a walk in the woods.

Damn, I loved that woman. Being without her at this stage of my life was never in the plan.

Nun's Island is located in the middle of the Saint Lawrence River, or *Le Fleuve Saint-Laurent* in correct *Québécois*. The island is home to twenty-five thousand people, just ten minutes from downtown.

It's a well-serviced residential community with a mix of middle-class apartments and townhouses, upscale luxury condos and large impressive homes among the trees and along the riverside. Many of the more expensive properties are owned by Montreal celebrities, NHL hockey players, media personalities and politicians.

The island has some jealously protected green space along the shoreline and around a small lake in the middle of the island. The lake and surrounding wetlands covered with mature maple, aspen and birch make the woods a popular destination for bird watchers and photographers. It's an appealing refuge from the city with its network of boardwalks and nature trails.

Dale felt that walking was pretty unambitious for an old athlete, but he had quit running marathons and ten-kilometer races in his mid-fifties, when his back and knees had started to complain.

He was in the woods on a chilly, damp November afternoon and as he came to the fork in the path, he was jolted out of the memories of that terrifying November day in 1988, when he and Susan had been threatened with kidnapping and murder.

She was so courageous through it all. God I miss her. We had more than thirty years together, through the good times and bad, and she won every battle she had to face. Except for the breast cancer.

Dale arrived at the dock on the shoreline of the lake. He stopped to look out at a heron, standing on long spindly legs in the shallow water by the shore, peering into the water for passing fish.

Good luck, buddy. No fun, fishing alone though, eh?

======

Part 4:

Back to Business

1988

35.

After Dale and Susan were well away from the sight of Frank's Caddy and the minivan jammed sideways on Rachel Street, Dale pulled into the parking lot off Camillien Houde Boulevard at the top of Mount Royal. They stopped against the curb, looking into the bare trees standing tall and dark above the brown leaves lying flat on the ground.

Dale got out quickly and went around to open the passenger door. He pulled Susan out of the car and silently held her close. She was trembling and tears streamed down her cheeks. She hugged him tightly and sobbed into his chest. There were only a few other cars parked in the lot and they were alone in a far corner.

"It's over, Susie, don't think about it anymore. You're safe now. We can talk about it later, when you're ready. Just take a few minutes here now to let it go. When you're ready, I'll call Pattie from the car and tell her we're on the way to pick up the kids."

Susan suddenly released him and looked up.

"Are they OK? Do they know what's happened?"

"Yes, they're OK. They're waiting for us with Pattie. I just told her you weren't home and to keep the kids after school until we get there. They don't know what's been going on. Neither does Pattie."

Susan calmed herself, took a few deep breaths and hugged him tightly again.

"OK, thank you, Dale. Thank you, thank you. My God, I don't know what would have happened, if you hadn't got me away from them."

She released him and stepped back toward the car. "Let's go home. I need to hug the kids."

*****

It had been a long, terrifying day. At home, they were now huddled close together on the sofa in the family room. Susan occasionally shuddered and fought back tears, as she described the events of her abduction and the fear of not knowing where she was or what was happening.

As she spoke, Dale's mind was flailing between worries for his family and seeking a way to stop Boncanno from ever coming after them again.

Sean and Keira were asleep upstairs, still unaware of the ordeal that their parents had just escaped from. Dale and Susan had agreed to tell them nothing of the events of the day.

They'll have enough nightmares of their own someday, without adding any of ours, Dale thought.

But what's next with these guys? Boncanno's a crazy, evil bastard and he's not going to stop, just because we got away again. Frank's obviously lost control of him.

Where the hell are they now? Plotting the next attempt on me and my family? There were three of them. Did the cops take them all away?

Frank had called from his Caddy earlier and reached them on Dale's phone in the BMW before they got home. He wanted to be sure that Susan was all right. He explained that he, too, had left the scene before the police arrived.

Safely at home now, Susan was recovering but still anxious. "Dale, we have to take this to the police. I know they told us not to do that, but we need to get them locked up. No more waiting for next time. Obviously, Frank can't protect us."

"I don't know. Looks like he saved us from Boncanno again. I never paid the ransom. Frank got to him somehow and I still have the hundred thousand cash in my briefcase."

He suddenly worried about it sitting in the front hall. He quickly got up and said, "Just a sec," before Susan could object. He brought the briefcase back into the family room and tucked it beside the end of the sofa, so he'd remember to take it upstairs and lock the cash in his desk drawer later.

"I'm not so sure about bringing the cops into it, Susan. These guys were pretty clear about that. I don't want them thinking about coming back again to stop us from calling the police."

"But you said Boncanno would never leave us alone until he's had his revenge," said Susan. "Now he's just going to be more determined."

"But like I told you before, Boncanno has a direct line to Detective Forsey and probably other dirty cops. He'll know right away, if we go to the police."

"Surely, there's at least one honest cop we can find to put him away."

"Hm-m-m, maybe," said Dale. "I'll talk to Frank. He might be in a position to help us finish this. Meanwhile, I think you and the kids should go up north and get out of town over the weekend."

Susan suddenly pulled away from him.

"No! I'm not running away and hiding. I want these guys put away! They should be running away and hiding. Not us! I don't want to jump out of my skin every time the doorbell rings."

"I know, I know, Susan. That's what I want too. I'd just like you to get away from here. Somewhere you can unwind a little from this ordeal and I can know that you and the kids are safe while I deal with this."

Susan moved further away on the sofa. She crossed her arms and took a long look at Dale before responding.

"OK," she sighed. "Maybe that's a good idea. I'll keep the kids home tomorrow and call to book the weekend up north. You can stay home with us too, until we know what we're doing. The kids will be happy to get an extra day off school."

"All right," said Dale. "I'll stay home until you're gone, then I'll go see Frank and we'll end this, once and for all."

"You said it yourself, Frank. This isn't over until Gino Boncanno is dead. So how do we make that happen? I'm ready to kill him myself, if that's what it takes."

They were sitting in Dale's BMW coupe and Frank filled the space on the passenger side, even though the seat was pushed well back.

"Dale, you're way out of your depth, talking murder now. Just lie low for a while and let the cops take care of Gino."

"Absolutely not. I'm not waiting for him to come back after us again. This time we have to move first and take care of him, before he has a chance to try again. No goddamn way am I going to leave my wife and kids out in the open, while he's still on the loose. We're dealing with a murderous madman here, Frank. We have to be just as ruthless as he is and remove him from the picture altogether. If he has to be dead for us to be safe, that's what I want."

Dale gripped the steering wheel with his left hand and turned toward Frank. He pounded his clenched fist on the centre console to punctuate each angry statement.

"I know I'm not the one to do it, Frank. Maybe you don't want to kill him either, so I'll pay whatever it takes to get somebody else to make him disappear, permanently. What about your new Mafia friends? Doesn't Lucky Luciano do that kind of thing?"

"He does, Dale. He takes care of his enemies if he has to, but he's not for hire by guys like you. Trust me, you don't even want to start down that path. You're talking crazy, Dale. You don't have any business in this world of violent gangsters, definitely not in the business of killing somebody. You don't want to end up in jail yourself, do you? How is that going to help your family?"

Frank paused, shaking his head, as he looked with concern at Dale.

"I know you feel exposed and the kidnapping was terrifying for you and Susan, but we can end this the right way. That means helping the cops put him away. It seems to me kidnapping and attempted murder should be enough to put him away for a long time. Let's give the cops what they need to do that."

"I have no confidence in the cops," said Dale. "We both know that Boncanno has insiders working for him. He's been getting away with murder for years. It's not good enough to hand it to the cops and hope they're honest and smart enough to put him in jail for life. We have to look after it ourselves, Frank. You know that, too."

"Well, you're partly right, but not all Montreal cops are crooked and stupid. You've met Hélène. She's smart and just as determined as you to put guys like Boncanno in jail. Before you think any more about doing something really stupid yourself, let me talk to her and see what she can do."

Dale fumed and gripped the steering wheel with both hands.

"I'll give you 'till Monday," he said. "Susan and the kids are with me up north until then. If you don't have better answers by Monday, I'm pushing you to find a way take care of it. No more screwing around, trying to be polite gentlemen. We need to be ruthless bastards, like they are."

"OK, OK. I'll see Hélène tonight and we'll look after it for Monday. Go unwind with your wife and kids, Dale. It's cool and quiet up North and you need to cool off, man. Don't even think about this stuff until I see you again Monday."

Frank opened the door and stepped out to walk across the parking lot outside 3D Computers to his Caddy parked at the end of the row of vehicles.

37.

Neither Hélène nor Frank enjoyed cooking. They both avoided the pressure of making meals for each other at home. They had their favourite spots for dinner together, where they could enjoy their privacy away from the world of crime and violence that otherwise occupied their time and attention.

Frank had a large old-fashioned apartment in Plateau Mont Royal in the heart of Montreal and Hélène had a modern condo in the residential development of Ile Paton in Laval, just north of Montreal. Tonight they were in the Salon des Voyageurs dining room of the Hotel du Nord in Laval. They had finished dinner and were near the end of their bottle of red wine.

Frank poured the last drops into Hélène's glass.

"So, do you think you have enough to arrest the three of them and keep them away from Dale Hunter and his family for a long time?"

Hélène looked serious.

"There's always a risk that we can't keep them in custody. Maybe they'd get out on bail, but then we could keep the Hunters under protection, if necessary. Let me put the pieces together to build a case. Then I'll try get an arrest warrant and make sure the judge knows why we need to keep Boncanno and his henchmen in custody until they can be tried and put away permanently. Don't forget I've been building a file on Boncanno for a while. Now, kidnapping will bump it up to the top of the list for the prosecutor. If we can make a charge of attempted murder stick, even better. Do you think Mrs. Hunter could I.D. the two who held her hostage? Maybe I can get one, or both of them, to admit it was all Gino's idea, in the first place. If we can line up all those pieces, I should be able to put him away for a while."

"What about my part in this little adventure?"

"Well, that might be a problem. You don't want me to come after you for kidnapping Gino's little boy, do you?"

"That wasn't kidnapping, just a little babysitting by my sister, while I negotiated with Gino."

"Gino, might tell it differently, but I don't think it gives him much of a defence. I'd prefer to keep you out of it. However, you might want to have a good lawyer standing by, in case I show up with handcuffs, next time I come to your place."

"Hmmm, that could be interesting. Let me settle up here, then we can go to your place and practice your technique with handcuffs."

"Frankie, that's a very evil suggestion. Shame on you."

"Yeah. Well, evil can be fun sometimes."

They left for Hélène's apartment nearby, both quietly contemplating the pleasures of an evening that would continue long into the night.

38.

Hélène decided to leave Frank out of the picture for the next steps. She contacted Dale at the cottage up north where he was with his family for the weekend. They made arrangements to meet at Station 21 downtown, on Monday morning.

"You'll remember that was where we first met, about a year ago," she said to Dale. "You came in to help us build a case against Jacques Talbot for the murder of André Lebeau. We agreed that the real criminal we needed to put away then was Gino Boncanno. Maybe this time we can do it."

"Oh, I remember," said Dale. "Too bad we couldn't put Boncanno away, because he tried very hard to get at me and my family again. My wife is terrified he's not done yet. So let's finish the job this time."

"I think we can put him away for a long time, if we can convict him on kidnapping. But I already have enough on him to make something stick. I'll see you on Monday. Please bring your wife and I'll try to reassure her that your troubles with Gino Boncanno are soon going to be over."

On Monday, Dale brought Susan to Station 21. It did bring back memories of his last visit. He set them aside and guided Susan gently into an interview room and introduced her to Detective Hélène Bourassa.

Initially, Susan was a bit nervous and tentative, but she was soon won over by the calm confidence of Hélène, as she explained the process and what was required of Susan to build a strong case against Boncanno.

Dale watched them building rapport.

Lookout, Boncanno, this tag team of tough young ladies is going to nail your ass and get you out of our lives forever.

Hélène explained the plan.

"I'd like you to look at some mug shots to identify the two who held you in captivity. I think we know who they are, since Gino uses the same two guys for a lot of his dirty work, but I need you to pick them out from the photos, then confirm your identification in a line-up when I bring them in. Is all that going to be OK with you?"

"Will I have to see them face to face, again?" asked Susan.

"Not unless you have to be called as a witness in open court and I don't think that will be necessary. I expect they'll plead guilty and blame it all on Gino in exchange for a lighter sentence. They don't want to face a kidnapping and conspiracy to commit murder charge themselves."

"Murder?" said Susan with a startled look from Hélène to Dale. "Who was talking about murder? And who were they planning to murder?"

"Sorry, Susie," said Dale, reaching over to squeeze her shoulder. "I didn't want to scare you any more, but we all think Gino probably intended to use the ransom demand to get me alone and then finish what he tried to do the last time. If we can prove that with the testimony of his henchmen, we'll really have him."

"My God, Dale, how did you ever get mixed up with these guys? They're dangerous people!"

"I know, I agree. Believe me, it was never my choice. It was just the luck of the draw and they pulled out my card. It all started with the demands for protection money. You know the story."

"Yeah, I know the story. I hope this will be the end of it."

She was no longer afraid, now she was angry and determined.

"OK, let's get started," said Hélène.

*****

The next day, early in the morning, four police officers arrived at the house on De Lorimier Street and picked up Pietro Lombardi and his partner Danny McBride, who had helped with the abduction. They were taken in handcuffs, in two separate police cars, downtown to Station 21.

At the same hour, an unmarked police car pulled up at the Vida da Vinci restaurant and Hélène Bourassa got out, followed by a young uniformed officer who had been driving, and another tall young detective in a grey wool topcoat.

Hélène was clearly in charge. She walked in the door past the two seated bodyguards, flashing her badge. They stood and watched her approach the door to Gino's office, but didn't interfere.

Hélène knocked once and walked in on Gino, who had been dozing in his shirtsleeves with his suit jacket stuffed behind his head against the high back of his chair. His stocking feet were crossed on the desktop. Startled by the interruption, he nearly fell out of the chair. He struggled to his feet and looked at the people standing in his doorway.

"What the hell," he started to object, then he saw the police badge extended by Hélène Bourassa.

"Gino Boncanno, you're under arrest for kidnapping and forcible confinement, conspiracy to commit murder and a long list of other charges that I'll read out to you at the station. Let's go."

She signalled to the young officer, who stepped forward and pulled out the handcuffs from behind his back.

"Wait, wait," said Gino, "my shoes...." His voice trailed off, as he slumped back in his chair. He pulled his shoes on quickly and tied the laces, then he reached for the suit jacket that had fallen on the floor.

Hélène waited for him to stand and pull on his jacket and straighten his tie. She turned and held the door for the officer to bring Gino out to the car.

Back at the station, she would start to play her cards, now that all the players were assembled there.

39

It was the end of a long day and the setting sun was reflecting off the windows of Station 21 into Saint Catherine Street and the heavy downtown traffic. Inside the station, Detective Hélène Bourassa was at her desk reviewing the notes from her interrogations of both Pietro Lombardi and Danny McBride.

They had separately and independently admitted that Gino was behind the kidnapping and that he had fully intended for them to kill Dale Hunter, when they got him alone. They were supposed to make it look like a mugging for the ransom money. Neither could say exactly what was planned for Susan, but Pietro, in particular, was willing to transfer as much blame as he could to Boncanno, since he had been so incompetent as to let them get caught and be identified by the intended victims.

Hélène collected the notes and stuffed them into a file folder. She carried her notebook and the folder down the hall and went into the interview room where Gino sat with his lawyer beside him.

Gino was looking relaxed. He was confident he could deal with this young lady cop, just as easily as he had with all the other cops that had tried to put him in jail. He was dismayed that his best paid resource in the Montreal police force, Detective Pierre Forsey, had not warned him of the arrest in advance. But he would deal with Forsey later, as soon as he got out of here. He didn't know that Hélène and some of the others working in the organized crime unit had their suspicions about Pierre Forsey and deliberately kept him in the dark on their investigations.

The lawyer beside Gino had been here before, too. The quality and style of his clothing and the slick haircut suggested he was making a good living at keeping his disreputable clients out of jail. He looked up at Hélène as she came in and gave her a tight-lipped smile.

Hélène dropped the thick folder on the table top between them, then sat down and opened her notebook.

She was followed into the room by her colleague in a rumpled brown wool suit with his plaid tie pulled loose from his neck. He was a tall young man with long blonde curly hair that made him look more like a visiting California surfer than a Montreal police detective. He sat and folded his arms across his chest looking at Gino and waiting for the proceedings to start.

The lawyer spoke first.

"My client has nothing more to say. I just need you to confirm the charges, if you have any. Then I can work on getting him out of here tonight, so he can go home to his family, like the rest of you." The tight smile reappeared.

Hélène ignored him and continued looking directly at Gino. "I don't need your client to say anything at all. I just want him to listen, so he knows what will happen next. He's not going home anytime soon."

Gino frowned back at her and leaned forward to put his elbows on the table, exaggerating his complete attention to her every word. The weak fluorescent ceiling lights reflected off the brown dome of his bald head fringed by grey hair. The lights made his head look like a big yellow Easter egg sitting in a white nest.

Hélène shook off the image.

"Gino, you should have stayed retired after the Renaldis shut you down last year," she said. "You might have stayed out of the trouble you're in now. As soon as you went back into business, we had you under surveillance again. We've had a wiretap on your office at the Vida da Vinci Restaurant and another at the house your guys have been using on De Lorimier, for the past six months."

Gino was still frowning, but now sat back and folded his arms across his chest, mirroring the young blonde detective sitting opposite his lawyer.

The three men looked at Hélène, as she continued.

"We have a tape of your conversations last week with Pietro Lombardi and Danny McBride, from both ends. So it's going to be pretty hard to deny you were in charge of the kidnapping of Mrs. Hunter."

Gino loosened his tie and ran his finger around the inside of his collar.

"And the murder charges are pretty solid, too," added Hélène. "We have the tape of your call telling them to call it off, but then a few minutes later, you made a second call and changed your mind. Something about the Hunters 'not getting out of this alive,' in pretty strong language, Gino. That's when Lombardi and McBride decided to bail out on you. They didn't want any part of your murder plans. They were just hoping to grab Hunter's money, drop his wife and leave you holding the empty bag."

Gino slammed his fist on the table and exploded.

"What about the black bastard who kidnapped my kid?"

Hélène looked back at him, calmly.

"Sorry, no recording of that. I don't know what you're talking about. But, you should also know, we have signed confessions from your two kidnappers and their testimony that you intended to kill Mr. Dale Hunter and, probably, his wife too. We do know you tried once before to kill him, right Gino? Your old buddy, Jacques Talbot, screwed it up that time. He's now in jail for another murder he did for you."

Gino was breathing hard and sweating. He leaned back in his chair with his arms crossed again.

Hélène continued.

"So to answer your lawyer's question, you're being charged with kidnapping and forcible confinement, plus conspiracy to commit murder. That should be enough to put you away for the rest of your life. We already had a long list of other charges against you, so if we stack them all together, you could be in jail for several lifetimes. The Crown prosecutor really likes what she's seen, so far, and is looking forward to an easy conviction on all counts. So you don't have to do anything, Gino. You're not leaving here tonight, or ever, so I hope you already said goodbye to your family."

She nodded to her colleague. "We're done here."

She picked up her notebook and the file folder. They both got up and walked out. The door closed behind them, followed by a noticeable loud click, as the lock was turned by the officer outside. He peered in through the small glass window and then backed away.

Gino leaned forward with his elbows on the table and put his head in his hands.

His lawyer looked very discouraged.

40.

"This is a rare pleasure and a first for the four of us," said Dale. "Getting together strictly for pleasure, no business issues and no crimes being committed."

He raised his glass in a toast to Susan, Frank and Hélène. "Thank you all for helping to get us here."

"Let's keep it this way," added Susan.

They clinked glasses and sipped the dark red wine. They were sitting together at the historic Beaver Club Restaurant of the Queen Elizabeth Hotel in the heart of downtown Montreal, a few weeks after the successful conviction and sentencing of Gino Boncanno.

"It's great to relax and enjoy life once in a while," said Frank. "Thank you, Dale, for arranging this celebration!"

"It's my pleasure. Let's hope it's not too long before we do this again. Because next time, it's on your tab, Frank."

"OK, but I'm not sure I'll be able to afford this kind of fine dining. Just a poor refugee kid from Somalia, remember."

"Ha!" said Dale. "He's negotiating already and the poor kid is doing better than any of us."

The two ladies looked at each other, shaking their heads.

"They just never quit," said Hélène.

The Beaver Club was originally the meeting place for the wealthy Montreal businessmen who ran the fur trade, Canada's first major industry from about 1620 until the mid-1800s. The Queen Elizabeth Hotel, of course, was known in French as *Le Reine Elizabeth.*

Dale enjoyed explaining the weirdness of the translation. "The Queen, *La Reine* in French, is translated to the masculine, *Le Reine,* only in Montréal. Because she's a hotel and it's grammatically correct!" He found it an amusing bilingual play on words. Not everyone got it.

The stately old Queen Elizabeth Hotel is prominently located in the city centre, opposite the modern landmark, Place Ville Marie with its 47-storey aluminum clad office tower on René Lévesque Boulevard. The boulevard had been recently renamed, in a very controversial decision by the Mayor of Montreal, Jean Doré, as a tribute to the separatist Premier of Quebec, René Lévesque, who had died the previous year, 1987.

For over one hundred and fifty years, the street had been known as Dorchester Boulevard, named after Lord Dorchester, the British Governor of Canada in the 1820s. Anglo Montrealers, who hated the separatist movement, also hated the name change to René Lévesque Boulevard.

Susan turned from Hélène to interrupt Dale and Frank's banter. "I hear you're getting licensed as a Private Investigator, Frank," she said. "That should keep you out of trouble a little, right?"

"Only if he doesn't get greedy," said Hélène. "He's not good at playing by the rules and too often the money's better, if he's breaking a few."

"I learned that from Dale," said Frank, giving him a nod. "He works way too hard trying to make an honest buck, just because he's not willing to break a few rules."

"Yeah, but I worry less," said Dale. "My way, it's simple. Just keep sales up and costs down. That makes everybody happy. And no need for me to hide anything from the auditors or the police."

"Yeah, and I love him more for doing it the hard way," added Susan, squeezing Dale's arm.

"And how is business these days, Dale?" asked Frank.

"Still good," said Dale, "but I'm looking at maybe a merger or acquisition. The competition keeps getting bigger, so I need to do the same. I'm looking for some new partners to work with, maybe a business to buy."

Hélène interrupted by clinking her spoon gently on her wine glass.

"OK, you guys, enough talk about business. Let's get back to *la joie de vivre* and enjoy the good life in Montreal. Especially the pleasure of dining in this historic establishment."

She held up the heavy leather-bound menu. "Have you looked at this menu? Too many choices!"

They all nodded agreement and set aside the distractions to open their menus.

THE END

AN INTRODUCTION TO THE NEXT NOVEL IN THE DALE HUNTER SERIES:

MERGER MANIAC

Some offers have to be refused

MERGER MANIAC is the third in the series of Dale Hunter crime novels, about an entrepreneur in the computer business of the 1980s. The business has grown rapidly and Hunter has done very well in spite of some attempts by the Montreal Mafia and the Triads of Taiwan to interfere and threaten violence against him and his family.

Now Hunter is trying to fight off the ruthless competitors coming after his business, as the industry rapidly evolves and it seems only the biggest will survive. He is seeking to make his own business bigger with a merger or the acquisition of another business. In his search for new partners, he is introduced again to the Renaldis, an aggressive and violent Montreal Mafia family, who loaned Hunter money in the past, when he was desperate to save his business. Now they're back, seeking Hunter's participation in their money laundering schemes.

Hunter is determined to refuse their offer, but they have very persuasive tactics for getting him to join them.

....

A PERSONAL NOTE TO READERS

This novel, SIMPLY THE BEST, is the second in the series of Dale Hunter crime thriller novels. I hope you found it an interesting and entertaining read and that you will try another novel in the Dale Hunter series. My intent with each novel is to share a few lessons of life and business, while adding some fascinating facts about Montreal and the technology of the 1980s.

The first novel, NO EASY MONEY, introduced the characters, the background and the initial plot lines. The stories continue in this novel and in MERGER MANIAC, to be published later this year.

The Dale Hunter series got started about fifteen years ago with some wild ideas in my head about stories from my own history as an entrepreneur in Montreal. Those ideas became the source of my initial scratchings in a notebook in 2015. Two and a half years later the series was launched.

I am dedicated to sharing my experience, ideas and advice to inspire and promote enlightened entrepreneurship and to help entrepreneurs be better and do better, for themselves and their families, their employees, customers and suppliers, their communities and the planet.

I hope you enjoy the stories and share them with your friends. Please post and share your review comments and tell me and other readers what you think. It helps us all to make better decisions about what to read and what to write.

You're also invited to visit my Author website and join the Reader Review Panel mailing list to keep in touch and receive advance notice of my next novels and other writing projects. Please visit:

DelvinChatterson.com or

LearningEntrepreneurship.com

Many thanks for your continued interest and support of my writing. Enjoy your reading.

Delvin Chatterson
Montreal, Canada,
March 2019

THANK YOU & ACKNOWLEDGEMENTS

First and most importantly, thank you to all the readers who took a chance on SIMPLY THE BEST being worth the time and money and making it all the way to the last page with me.

All my novels and business books are inspired by the real-life stories of entrepreneurs and business associates whom I have worked with during the last thirty years and more. I sincerely thank them all for sharing their stories with me.

The quality of this novel has been greatly enhanced by the active support and feedback from early readers, reviewers and editors, especially friends and family, who continually cheer me on and inspire me to make it better. Better than polite compliments, they tell me what they really think of the early drafts and contribute greatly to the success of the novels.

Then they recommend them to their friends! The full list of collaborators and supporters is available at my Author website <u>DelvinChatterson.com</u>.

The outstanding covers for the first three novels are the work of Caroline Teagle. Final editing and review has been done by Allister Thompson. The book design and publishing were the work of the team of helpful experts at Tellwell Talent. Any remaining deficiencies are all mine and I look forward to you pointing them out. It all helps the next one!

I have tried to make each of these novels a fun family project with inspiration and input, critique and commentary from my grandsons, Lucas and Michael, my children Kim and Jon, and my patient and loving wife, Penny. I know it hasn't always been fun.

Thank you all!

Delvin Chatterson
Montreal, Canada,
March 2019

THE AUTHOR
DEL CHATTERSON

Like Dale Hunter, Del Chatterson is an engineer from UBC with an MBA from McGill and he ran a computer products distribution business in Montreal in the 1980s.

Some of the stories in the Dale Hunter Series actually happened, most are fiction. "These are my worst nightmares," he says, "that I decided to share through these novels."

Del started his own business, called TTX Computer Products, in 1986 and grew it to $20 million-a-year in sales with distribution centres in Montreal and Boston. He then took it into a merger to expand the business across Canada. The merger was eventually wound-up amid the rapid decline of independent businesses and consolidation of the major players in the computer industry.

Del is a strategic advisor, consultant, coach and cheerleader for entrepreneurs and has written extensively on business topics for decades. In addition to this series of Dale Hunter crime thriller novels, Del is also working on a short story collection and new editions of his two previously published business books, **Don't Do It the Hard Way**, *A wise man learns from the mistakes of others, only a fool insists on making his own,* and **The Complete Do-It-Yourself Guide to Business Plans,** *It's about the process, not the product.*

Originally from the Rocky Mountains of British Columbia, Del has lived and worked for most of the past forty years in the fascinating, multicultural, bilingual, French-Canadian city of Montreal, Quebec.

Del has helped entrepreneurs around the world, including volunteer consulting and financial support in developing economies and in Aboriginal communities. His own life experience includes running nine marathons after the age of fifty (setting no records, but never being last) and running for Member of Parliament in the 2000 Canadian Federal election. (He came second, not last.)

Learn more about Del at his Author website for readers at: <u>DelvinChatterson.com</u> and more of his advice for entrepreneurs at: <u>LearningEntrepreneurship.com</u>. You may also follow Del on Twitter, Facebook, Instagram or LinkedIn.

Thank you for sharing his books and providing your feedback, comments and reviews. Del welcomes any opportunity to connect with readers.

*****